Annie Oakley

Young Markswoman

Illustrated by Jerry Robinson

Annie Oakley

Young Markswoman

By Ellen Wilson

Aladdin Paperbacks

Aladdin Paperbacks
An imprint of Simon & Schuster
Children's Publishing Division
1230 Avenue of the Americas
New York, NY 10020
Copyright © 1958, 1962 by the Bobbs-Merrill Company, Inc.
All rights reserved including the right of reproduction
in whole or in part in any form.
First Aladdin Paperbacks edition, 1989
Printed in the United States of America

10   9   8   7

Library of Congress Cataloging-in-Publication Data
Wilson, Ellen Janet Cameron.
Annie Oakley: young markswoman/by Ellen Wilson.—1st Aladdin
Books ed.
        p.   cm. — (The childhood of famous Americans series)
Reprint. Originally published: Annie Oakley: little sure shot.
Indianapolis: Bobbs-Merrill, 1958.
Summary: Focuses on the childhood of the famous American
sharpshooter.
ISBN 0-689-71346-0
1. Oakley, Annie, 1860-1926—Childhood and youth—Juvenile
literature.   2. Shooters (of arms)—United States—Biography—
Juvenile literature.   3. Entertainers—United States—Biography—
Juvenile literature.   [1. Oakley, Annie, 1860-1926—Childhood and
youth.   2. Sharpshooters.   3. Entertainers.]   I. Title.
II. Series.
GV1157.03W55   1989
799.3'092—dc20   [B]   [92]   89-37820   CIP   AC

For Kathie

Illustrations

Full pages

Numerous smaller illustrations

Contents

★   ★

★ Annie Oakley

Young Markswoman

Girls Don't Go Hunting

ANNIE PUT DOWN the scissors and a piece of newspaper. "Here's a string of paper dolls for you, Hulda," she said as she unfolded a long row of little paper figures. She held them out to her three-year-old sister. "See," she chanted. "They're going hunting to get a little rabbit skin to wrap the baby Hulda in."

Hulda gave a cry of delight. She ran across the rough cabin floor to take the paper dolls in her chubby hands.

The string of ten cutouts was joined together by hands holding tiny rifles. From each paper head two little pigtails hung down. There was a paper hair ribbon on each one, and the skirts looked as if they were blowing in a breeze.

Elizabeth, an older sister, looked at the dolls admiringly. "My, you're quick with scissors, Annie. Nobody else in all of Ohio could make such good cutouts so fast. And the guns are best of all—they're just like Father's rifle."

"Do you really think so?" Annie asked eagerly. She looked at the long rifle hanging over the fireplace.

Sarah Ellen, another older sister, looked up from her work. She was tying sassafras roots into bundles for her mother. Mother was away taking care of a sick neighbor. "Yes, the guns are good," Sarah Ellen said. "But why did you make girl dolls? If they're holding guns they ought to be boys. Girls don't go hunting. They don't even go to shooting matches."

"Why don't they?" Annie asked. "I think it would be fun. I'd like to go to a shooting match someday, too. Lyda's friend Joe Stein says it's really good sport."

Lyda, the oldest sister, spoke quickly. "Yes, it's good sport for men—and boys, too. But Joe says girls don't know how to handle guns. That's why men don't want women at their shoots. Or girls, either." Lyda's needle wove in and out of the stocking she was mending. "Girls are supposed to stay home and sew and keep house and do useful things like that."

Annie made a comical face. "I guess keeping house and sewing are useful, but there are lots of times when I'd rather be outdoors. I'd be out right now if the rain would stop."

"Me, too," her brother Johnny chimed in.

"Hunting is useful, too," Annie went on. "Remember those rabbits that steal food from our garden? The squirrels take our black walnuts, too. Someone ought to go after them with a gun." Annie grabbed the hearth broom and aimed at an imaginary squirrel up near the ceiling. "Bang!" she cried. "Bang! Bang!"

Johnny was quick to enter the game. "You got him!" he shouted.

Annie ran over and pretended to pick up the animal. "Squirrel pie for supper!" She smacked her lips hungrily.

The sisters smiled. Elizabeth said, "You're making me hungry."

Annie sighed. "If only it were a real squirrel! If only I could use our real gun!"

"Why, Annie, you could hardly lift Father's gun," Lyda answered. "It's bigger than you are. You're no bigger than a minute, even if you are seven years old."

Annie stood on tiptoe. She stretched as tall as she could. "See? I'm not so little."

Johnny ran over and stood beside Annie. He stretched on tiptoe, too. "I'm only five, but I'm almost as tall as Annie," he said.

14

Annie gave her brother a hug. "Of course you are. Even if we can't have squirrel for supper, we'll both have extra helpings of bread and milk tonight. Then we'll both grow bigger."

Lyda laughed. Then she sighed. "I'm afraid there won't be extra helpings for any of us after a while. Mother says we may have to sell Old Pink to get some money."

"Sell our cow!" Annie cried. "Why?"

Lyda sighed again. "Mother can't make enough money nursing. She never gets more than a dollar and a quarter a week."

The children were quiet. They could hear the rain dripping on the roof of the little log cabin. They thought of the sad winter a few years before, when their strong, cheerful father became ill and died.

"Come now," Lyda said briskly. "It's time to get everything ready for Mother when she comes home. I'll get more logs for the fire."

"I'll go out to the shed and milk Old Pink," Sarah Ellen offered.

"I'll straighten up the room," said Elizabeth. "Hand me the rest of that newspaper you cut up, Annie. I'll save it to make a dress pattern someday. I'm glad our neighbor gave the paper to Mother last week. We don't see one often."

Annie looked at the paper closely. "I wish I could read it," she said. "If the schoolhouse weren't so far away, I could go to school and learn to read. What paper is it? What does it say, Lyda?"

"It's the Cincinnati *Daily Gazette*. Up here is the date, October 22, 1867. I'll read you some of it tonight."

Annie took one more look at the puzzling print before she handed the paper to Elizabeth. Then she looked out the window. Her face brightened. "Look, it's almost stopped raining! I'm going outdoors to gather some nuts before the squirrels get them. The squirrels have been mighty busy lately."

"Me, too," Johnny said.

"Tag along if you want to," Annie replied.

"Tag Along!" Lyda said. "That's a good name for Johnny. Everywhere Annie goes, Johnny tags along."

Two Birds in a Tree

ANNIE TOOK A deep breath. "It's stuffy indoors," she said to Johnny. "Outdoors is much nicer." She glanced around at their little Ohio farm. Most of the leaves had fallen in the late October rains. Now they lay scattered on the ground, where they looked like a soft red and yellow carpet. The leaves made squishy sounds as the two started to walk through them.

Then Annie heard another sound. She cocked her head to listen. "What was that?"

"What was what?" Johnny asked.

"Sh!" Annie put a finger to her lips. For a minute all was still. Then a shot rang out.

"What's going on?" Annie wondered aloud. "Come on, Johnny, let's go see."

With Johnny at her heels, Annie ran toward the woods. Soon there was the sound of another shot, followed by more cheering. The sounds grew louder. Horses whinnied and men shouted.

Annie and Johnny ran in and out among the trees when they reached the woods. They did not slow down until they reached the edge of a clearing. Annie stopped so suddenly that Johnny bumped into her. She stepped behind a big beech tree and pulled Johnny with her. "Don't let them see us," she whispered.

Annie and Johnny peeked around the tree. There, at the far end of the large, level clearing, were about twenty men. Each one had a gun. They were all clustered about a huge oak tree, laughing and looking at something.

Annie's sharp eyes saw two small shingles nailed to the oak tree. "Those shingles are their targets. They're having a shoot," she said. "Quick! Now's our chance." She swung herself up into the beech tree. Johnny swung himself up after her.

"Now we can see everything," Annie said, "but we mustn't let them see us. Remember, Lyda says men don't want women and children around at a shoot. Especially women. I guess women are always scared of being hurt."

"Well, we're not women!" Johnny exclaimed in a loud whisper.

Annie giggled. "We're not scared, either." She tossed her braids back over her shoulders.

A loud "gobble, gobble, gobble" came from the ground.

Annie and Johnny were so startled that they almost fell from their perches. When they got their balance again, they saw the gobbler. He was a huge turkey penned up in a large wooden box in some nearby bushes. The two watched him stretch his long neck up between the slats of the box. They looked at his sharp beak and his snapping black eyes.

"Isn't he fierce!" Johnny said.

"Yes. He must be the prize at this turkey shoot," Annie said.

"Gobble, gobble, gobble!" The turkey gave a harsh cry again. The men paid no attention. They looked first at one target, then the other.

"Look, Annie, there's Joe, Lyda's friend. See?" Johnny pointed across the field.

"Yes, and there's Mr. Shaw, too. Remember the time he came to get Mother when his family was sick?"

Joe was measuring something carefully on two of the targets. Finally he called out, "It's a tie! A tie between Duncan and Shaw. Each man has a bull's-eye. Each has two other hits inside the circle. They're exactly the same distance from the bull's-eye."

A cheer went up from the group.

"That means there will be another round between Duncan and Shaw," Joe said. "The winner takes home the turkey!"

Everybody cheered again and began to move away from the target tree.

Annie grabbed Johnny. "They're going to shoot again!" she cried in her clear, high voice. "We'll see who wins the turkey!" In her excitement she forgot to be quiet. Too late she clapped her hand over her mouth.

The men had heard her. The one nearest their tree looked up. "Well, look up there!" he shouted, as he pointed to their tree. "That's the strangest pair of birds I ever did see." Everyone looked up into the tree.

Annie and Johnny said nothing. They sat perfectly still.

Lyda's friend Joe came over. He grinned. "If I'm not mistaken, one of them's an Annie-bird.

The other one's a Johnny-bird, sure as shootin'. They're Mrs. Moses' young ones."

Annie called down from her perch, "We've never seen a shoot before. Please let us stay and see who wins the turkey!"

Joe said, "How about it, Mr. Shaw?"

Mr. Shaw, an older man, looked up at Annie. Her big, gray eyes were eager. Finally he said, "Oh, let them stay. They're safe up there. As long as they keep quiet, they won't bother anyone, I guess."

Annie smiled her thanks. She and Johnny would keep quiet all right—as quiet as bumps on a log.

Everyone lined up to watch. Duncan was to shoot first. He lay down on his stomach behind a small log. Carefully he rested the muzzle of his gun on the log and pressed the butt of the gun against his shoulder. He and the gun were well braced and steady.

Everyone was quiet. Johnny and Annie scarcely breathed.

"Bang!"

Annie kept her eyes open, but this time she kept her mouth shut.

Down by the target tree, Joe called out, "A bit to the right of center!"

Now the second and third shots. "Center!" Joe called both times.

"Hurrah for Duncan!" the men yelled. "It won't be easy to beat that, Shaw!"

How exciting it all was! Imagine being able to hit the center of a small target like that! Annie wanted to yell, too, but she remembered she must not make a sound.

Now Mr. Shaw took his place. He was going to stand up to shoot. Annie hoped he would win. He raised his gun to his shoulder while the men stood like statues. Annie and Johnny sat motionless in their tree.

Mr. Shaw took quick aim and fired. "Center!" cried Joe.

Twice more Mr. Shaw fired.

Joe called, "Center!" And again, "Center!"

The crowd of men cheered and clapped the winner on the back. Horses neighed. Annie and Johnny climbed down out of the tree, as nimble as two squirrels.

Annie went over to Mr. Shaw. "Yes siree," Duncan said. "That makes Shaw the best shot in all of Darke County."

Annie pulled on the winner's coat. Mr. Shaw leaned down to listen.

"I'm glad you won the turkey," she said, "and thank you for letting us stay." Then she and Johnny raced toward home.

At supper that evening Annie and Johnny filled up their bowls a second time with bread, milk, and maple sugar. "So we can grow faster," Annie said.

As Johnny took his last bite, he looked up at his mother. "Am I bigger yet?"

Everybody laughed. Mother answered him in her soft Quaker speech. "Thee is growing just right for a five-year-old." Then she turned to Annie. "What did thee do today, child?"

"Tag and I went to a turkey shoot!"

"Tag?" Mother asked. "Who is Tag?"

The children looked at one another with sparkling eyes. "Tag Along! Tag Along Johnny!" Annie explained with a laugh.

Mother joined in the laughter. "There, thee has a new name, Johnny! I do believe it fits thee. But what's this about a turkey shoot?"

"Girls aren't supposed to go to turkey shoots! Annie, I told you that!" Lyda scolded.

"I didn't plan to go," Annie said. "But after we got there, Joe said we could stay. Mr. Shaw did, too. You should have seen Mr. Shaw shoot! He hit dead center three times in a row!" Annie's gray eyes shone in the lamplight. "I wish I could do that! If I could, we would all have roast turkey for supper."

Mother laughed. Then she sighed. "Father used to bring home turkeys. We always had roast turkey or quail for birthday dinners."

Lyda looked up. "Why, it's your birthday next week, isn't it, Mother? I almost forgot."

28

"We'll have no turkey or quail for Mother on this birthday," said Annie sadly. "I guess we'll just have mush."

"Maybe we will just have mush, but it will be such good mush, Annie!" Mother said cheerfully. "I won't complain. Now do tell us all about the turkey shoot, you two."

The Trap

THE NEXT DAY Annie and Lyda were busy in the little cabin. Annie was supposed to dust the furniture, but she was so busy talking about the turkey shoot that she forgot to dust.

Finally Lyda said, "Annie, try to make your tongue go a little slower. Then maybe you can make your dustcloth go a little faster. You are usually so quick, but today you are as slow as molasses. What will Mother say?"

Annie thought a minute. Then with a grin she said, "Mother will say, 'Annie, if you don't attend to the dusting, I will give that task to Johnny.'"

Lyda laughed. "Johnny with a dustcloth! Such a joke! Besides, Mother would say, 'If thee doesn't mind the dusting.' Even when she scolds, Mother doesn't sound cross with her gentle Quaker speech."

Annie nodded. Then she climbed up on a chair so she could dust the long shelf over the fireplace. She stared at her father's rifle. It hung just above the mantle.

The rifle wasn't dusty, but it wasn't shiny either. The beautiful curly maple wood of the stock was dull. Annie knew it was called "curly" maple because the grain of the wood made curly patterns. The brass star set in the gun for decoration was dull, too, and there was no shine on the long barrel.

"You know," Annie said finally, "all the guns at the shoot yesterday were shiny clean. Father's rifle would look just as good as they do if I polished it. Could I, Lyda?"

Lyda laughed. "Seems to me you're having a hard time today just getting the furniture polished. Besides, Joe always says the outside of a gun isn't so important as the inside. He swabs out the barrel of his rifle all the time."

"Well, I'll do the inside, too, if you'll show me how," Annie said.

"I guess it is about time for somebody to oil this one again. We shouldn't let it get rusty. The room must be dusted first, though."

Annie jumped down off the chair. She flew around the room with her dustcloth. In a short time she had dusted everything—even the bottom of the rockers on Mother's rocking chair. She shook the dustcloth out the door and hung it on its nail.

Sarah Ellen had been watching. "Well, Annie, you really did make the dust fly! Come on, Elizabeth, let's get the rifle down for her."

"I know it isn't loaded," Lyda said. "Just the

same, we've got to make sure." Lyda pushed the ramrod down the barrel of the gun. The rod went in all the way. "No ball or gunpowder there." She pulled the ramrod out.

Annie asked, "What kind of grease should we use for inside the barrel?"

"Oh, any kind that isn't salty. A bit of goose grease will do. Here. Put some on this little rag. Fasten the rag to the screw on the end of the ramrod. That's the way. Now watch."

Lyda took the rod and pushed it down the long barrel. She pushed and pulled to make the ramrod and the greasy rag go back and forth.

"Let me! Let me!" Annie cried.

"Yes, I'll hold the gun while you work the ramrod," Lyda replied.

Finally they were both satisfied that every speck of dust and lint had been oiled away.

"Now for the trigger and the hammer." Lyda went over these with a fresh oily rag.

"Let me try the trigger," Annie said. She pulled back the hammer. *Click!* She pulled the trigger. *Snap!*

Lyda nodded. "Slick as a whistle," she said. "Even Father couldn't have done better."

"I can do all the rest by myself—this outside part," Annie said. "What kind of grease do I use to shine the stock and barrel?"

Lyda laughed. "Mostly elbow grease. Just rub and polish, rub and polish."

"Let me help, Annie," Johnny begged.

"All right. Let's get down on the floor. We can work better there."

By the end of an hour, with a little help from Johnny, Annie had made the gun look like new. When it was hung up over the fireplace again, she stood back to admire it. The curly maple stock gleamed like satin. The star shone like gold. In the flickering light of the fire, the long barrel looked almost blue.

"Well, I must say that's the best it's looked for a long time," Lyda said. "I've never had time to give it more than a lick and a promise myself. You're a good worker, Annie."

Annie beamed. Then she stretched. "I've got kinks in my arms and legs from sitting still so long. Come on, Tag. Let's go outside and un-kink ourselves."

Annie and Johnny wandered into the corn-field. Only a few ragged cornstalks were left. As Annie passed one of them, she heard a rus-tling noise.

She grabbed Johnny's hand and whispered, "Listen! What's that?"

Out of the stubble came a warning whistle. "Bob *White!*" Then again, "Bob *White!*" With a rush of wings a flock of birds flew out of the stubble. They slanted off toward the woods.

"Turkeys!" Johnny cried. "Little turkeys!"

"No, not turkeys. Quail! They're smaller,

and you can tell them by their white necks and brown coats. They're just as good to eat as turkeys, though. I wish I could get one for Mother. That would be a real surprise for her birthday. I remember when Joe brought some to Lyda once. She roasted them. They were good!"

"Catch the quail!" Johnny said, as he started to run toward the woods.

Annie laughed and called him back. "They've gone too far by now. We couldn't catch them with our hands, anyhow. Joe said he trapped his with a trap made of cornstalks. I wonder how you make a cornstalk trap."

She stood still for a minute, thinking. She looked out over the few yellow stalks of corn left standing. "I can try, anyhow," she said suddenly. "Come, help me break off some cornstalks. Those quail will be back here sometime. Maybe we can have something ready for them when they come. A trap! Think of it, Johnny. If we could make a trap that would catch a quail! Then Mother would have a real birthday treat."

Annie and Johnny gathered a little pile of cornstalks. Annie went to work to break them into shorter pieces. Her hands were small, but they were strong and quick.

"Now, let's see," Annie said. "What should we do first? Begin like this, I guess."

Johnny watched while Annie laid four pieces of cornstalk in a square on the ground, one pair on top of the other pair. "That's about the right size. Now I'll put two more sticks across the two top ones at the corners, this way."

"Like a tic-tac-toe game," Johnny said.

"Yes. Now we'll just keep adding sticks to make it high."

"It's going to look like a tiny log cabin," Johnny said excitedly.

Annie stopped to look at it. "The trouble is, it isn't going to be steady enough. A quail could knock it to pieces easy as pie. I know! Do you have some string, Tag?"

Johnny pulled some tangled pieces of string from his pocket. Annie started over again. This time she tied the cornstalks tightly together at the corners. "That's better, but even if a quail couldn't get through the side, it could fly though the top. We'll have to cover it somehow," she said.

Annie thought a minute. "Let's push a whole row of cornstalks through, close together—just below the top rails. There. That makes a tight lid to the trap."

Johnny nodded. "Now the quail can't get out," he said with satisfaction.

Annie sat back to admire the trap. "I really think it will work," she said. She was so pleased with her invention that she jumped up and whirled around three times. Then she stopped suddenly and made a funny face.

"What's the matter?" Johnny asked.

"I've just thought of something. If the quail can't get out, how will it get inside in the first place?" Annie laughed. "Now what'll we do?"

Johnny looked hopeful. Surely Annie would think of something. She always did.

Annie was puzzled for just a minute. Then she said, "I've got an idea. Tag, go find an old ear of corn. I'll work on things here."

While Johnny was gone, Annie dug a little trench in the soft damp earth. She made the trench go uphill at one end. Johnny came running with an ear of corn and helped Annie get the grains off the cob. She let Johnny sprinkle corn all along the trench.

She put what was left in a single heap at the high end of the trench. Then, over the heap, she placed the trap. Carefully she propped up one end of the trap with a short stick. "See? The quail will knock down the stick. The trap will come down on top of him. Then he won't be able to get out!"

Annie straightened up. "Now, we'd better hide the trap from hungry animals. We don't want a fox or wolf to get our quail."

Johnny shivered a little.

Annie saw him shiver. Quickly she said, "Of course, wolves don't come around until winter, and foxes don't bother people. 'Coons or musk-rats or possums might like quail for supper, but so would Mother!"

"And so would we!" Johnny said, smacking his lips. He helped Annie gather brush. Together they heaped the branches lightly over the trap. Soon it was hidden from sight.

By now it was almost dark. On their way home, Johnny could not help thinking about wolves. He slipped his hand into Annie's. "Annie will take care of me," he thought. "She is never afraid of anything."

A silvery star shone over the woods. Annie pointed to it. "There's the North Star, Tag. See? It has the same name as the township we live in—North Star Township. Let's make a wish on it. Don't tell me what you wish, though, or it won't come true. Don't tell anyone about the trap, either. It's a secret. We want to surprise Mother on her birthday."

All Cocked and Ready to Shoot

NEXT MORNING Annie was the first one to open her eyes. She looked at Sarah Ellen beside her on the high feather bed. She was still asleep. In a second big bed, Lyda and Elizabeth were sound asleep, too. Mother stirred in her bed but did not waken. Baby Hulda, in her sleep, snuggled up closer to Mother.

Over in the trundle bed a tuft of brown hair was sticking out. That was all Annie could see of Johnny. He had burrowed under the blue and white quilts like a groundhog. Then Annie remembered the trap. She slid to the floor, tiptoed to the trundle bed, and gave Johnny's hair a tweak. Johnny popped up, his startled eyes wide open. Annie put a finger to her lips. "Secret," she whispered.

In no time they were dressed and in the kitchen. Both of them tugged at the strong bar that guarded the door every night. When it slid back, Annie lifted the door latch. It made a slight clicking sound. Outside, Annie shivered and took a deep breath. How beautiful it was this morning! The sun was red as it rose over the cornfield.

"Come on, Tag Along!" Annie caught Johnny's hand and started to run. Her heart beat fast. Had the trap worked? Would there be a quail inside?

They slowed down when they came to the rows of stubble. "Quiet," Annie said softly. "Let's walk like Indians." In single file they crept toward the trap.

"Look, Annie, the corn's still in the trench,"

Johnny whispered. "The quails must not have eaten any of it."

Annie nodded, frowning. Gently she lifted up some of the brush pile. The trap was empty! The corn lay untouched in its little heap under the cornstalk trap.

Annie was disappointed. So was Johnny.

"Never mind, Tag. It's too early for the quail, I guess. That's it. They haven't had time to find the corn yet. Come on. We'll go away so they'll come. We can look again tomorrow. It isn't Mother's birthday yet, anyhow."

The two trappers cheered up over their breakfast of johnnycakes and maple syrup. "My cakes," Johnny called them. He thought they were named for him.

Before Mother left for her day of nursing, she gave each of the children a job to do. Since the sun was bright and warm, the older girls were to wash the clothes. Annie and Johnny were to churn the butter. "We won't have butter much longer if we have to sell Old Pink," Mother said. "Churn as much as thee can."

"When we are through, may we take Hulda outside with us?" Annie asked.

Mother gave Annie's thick chestnut hair a loving pat. "Thee is never one to stay indoors, is thee, Annie? Yes, thee may take Hulda outside, but stay near the house with her."

The big sisters went off to the stream to wash the big basket of clothes. Annie and Johnny took turns pushing the churn handle up and down. Annie chanted the old riddle about a churn:

"What's big at the bottom, little at the top,
  With something in the middle that goes
    flippety-flop?"

Hulda trotted around the kitchen saying, "Flippety-flop, flippety-flop."

The two butter-makers worked until their arms ached. At last the butter was finished, sweet and fresh. Suddenly the children heard a horse and wagon coming down the lane. Who could it be? They rushed to the door to see. A man got down and tied his horse to a tree.

"It's Mr. Shaw!" Annie cried. "The best shot in Darke County!"

Mr. Shaw smiled at the little group in the doorway. Hulda peeked out at him from behind Annie's skirt.

"Where's your gun?" Annie asked.

"I'm not after wild game today," Mr. Shaw answered. "I've come to look at your cow."

Annie caught her breath. Were they going to lose Old Pink so soon? "Mother's away nursing," Annie said.

"I know. I saw her this morning and she told me the cow was for sale. She said I could come and see if I liked her."

Annie turned to her brother. "Tag, go find Old Pink," she said. "She's probably wandered off somewhere. Listen for her bell. I'll stay here with Hulda."

Annie remembered what Mother did when visitors came. She said to Mr. Shaw, "Come in and I'll make a fresh cup of tea."

This was the first time Annie had played lady of the house. She felt important. She stirred up the fire to make the kettle boil the way Mother and Lyda did when they had company. She ran over to the cupboard to get the good white cups.

"That looks like a mighty fine rifle up there," Mr. Shaw said. "Its barrel must be forty inches long. That's nice curly maple in the stock, too. How does the rifle shoot?"

Annie beamed. "Mother says Father thought it was fine. He bought it in Pennsylvania before he came to Ohio. Nobody's tried the rifle since he died."

"Well, without a man on the place, who keeps it polished up so nice?"

"When I saw the nice shiny guns at the shoot the other day, I decided to clean it. I did it yesterday. Lyda showed me how."

Mr. Shaw looked down in surprise. "Why, child, I don't recollect ever seeing a girl take that much notice of guns. You don't fire it, too, do you?" He laughed at the idea.

"No, it's never loaded. Mother says I'm too little. But I *could* shoot it. I just know I could."

Mr. Shaw started to laugh again at the thought that this little girl could fire a gun. Then he stopped at the sight of her eager face. Her eyes sparkled the way they had at the turkey shoot. Without another word Mr. Shaw took the rifle down off its pegs.

"The first rule about a gun is this: Always know for sure it isn't loaded," Mr. Shaw said.

"Lyda showed me how to ram the rod down in

49

the barrel to see if there's any powder or ball in it," Annie said.

"Yes, and another way is to pull the hammer back to make sure there's no cap there. This kind of rifle can't go off without a percussion cap, you know. Your mother wouldn't mind if I loaded it, I know. I've used a lot of guns."

He peered into the long blue barrel. "It looks clean," he said.

"It is. I swabbed it out, too."

"Any balls left in the pouch?" he asked.

Annie took the fringed shot bag down off its hook. "Yes, it's half full. There's powder in the powder horn, too. Here's the patch bag, too, Mr. Shaw."

Excitedly, Annie brought over the little leather bag which held the patches. Inside were some cloth patches made of linen. Tiny squares were stitched together to make larger squares. There were several percussion caps in the bag, too.

50

Annie took out a patch and a cap and handed them to Mr. Shaw.

Mr. Shaw slung the powder horn over his shoulder. "Do you have a measure for the powder?" he asked.

"No, Father didn't have one. I guess he always knew how much powder to put in."

"Well, I do, too. Let's load her up."

Hulda wasn't interested. She began playing with her paper dolls over in the corner. But Annie watched Mr. Shaw's every move. First he pulled the stopper out of the powder horn. Next he poured a little powder down into the muzzle of the gun. He didn't spill a single grain.

"Now for the patch and ball," he said. He spread the cloth patch across the opening of the muzzle. In the exact center of the patch he put the lead ball which was the bullet. This he pressed in with his thumb.

"Now for the ramrod." Mr. Shaw drew the

hickory rod out from the rings of brass that held it beneath the barrel. With the rod he pushed the bullet and its cloth covering down the barrel. Now the ball rested on the powder.

Next he pulled back the hammer, then asked Annie for a percussion cap. Annie handed him one. This he fitted under the hammer.

"There you are," he said. "When you grow used to a gun you can load it in twenty seconds. Now she's all cocked and ready to shoot."

Crack Went
the Rifle!

MR. SHAW took the rifle out the open doorway.
Annie reached eagerly for the gun, but Mr. Shaw
hesitated. He looked at her doubtfully. "You're
such a little thing I don't know whether you can
even lift it to your shoulder or not," he said. "Do
you think you can?"

"Let me try. Oh, please let me!"

Annie looked so eager that Mr. Shaw handed
her the rifle.

Annie took the gun. Carefully pointing it
toward the ground, she looked around for her
little sister. Hulda was in one corner of the
cabin, playing with her paper dolls.

"That's right, Hulda," Annie said. "You stay right there for a while."

Mr. Shaw watched with amazement as Annie swung the gun to her shoulder with natural grace. Her cheek, pink from excitement and from the effort of lifting the heavy gun, nuzzled against the stock. "What shall I shoot at?"

"See that walnut hanging on the bare branch over there? See how near you can come to hitting it," Mr. Shaw said.

Taking careful aim, Annie pulled the trigger. *Crack* went the rifle! Down came the walnut.

Annie laughed with delight.

Mr. Shaw whistled in astonishment. "You shoot like an old-timer! This surely isn't the first time you ever shot a rifle!"

Annie turned to him with sparkling eyes. "It is. Honest!"

"How did you know what to do?" Mr. Shaw asked. "Who told you?"

"Nobody. I just pulled the trigger when it felt like the right time."

Mr. Shaw shook his head. "Well, I never saw the like," he said in his deep voice. "Never in all my life."

Just then a clanging sound reached their ears. They turned to see Old Pink coming through the opening in the rail fence. Johnny ran behind her, with a switch in his hand. Hulda ran out the door of the cabin to meet them.

"I'll take my turn another day," Mr. Shaw said. "My cup of tea, too." He went over to look at Old Pink.

Annie leaned the rifle carefully against the cabin. "Now I'll get to clean it again," she thought happily to herself before following Mr. Shaw across the yard.

Mr. Shaw was soon satisfied with the cow's healthy look. "I'll take her," he said.

He tied the cow to the rear of his wagon. As

he climbed up onto the wagon seat, he said, "Your mother told me I could pay her at the place where she is working."

Johnny and Hulda looked at Old Pink. Johnny's freckled face was solemn. Little Hulda hid her face in Annie's skirt and began to cry. Annie knelt down beside her. "What's the matter, Hulda?"

"Don't let the man take Old Pink away!"

Annie smoothed back her sister's short curls. "It's all right, Hulda. Mother said he could."

Mr. Shaw looked troubled. "I'll send over some milk whenever I can," he promised. "How would you children like Old Pink's bell to keep? I have extra bells at home."

Hulda stopped crying and Johnny looked more cheerful. Annie hurried over, reached up, and unfastened the cowbell. "Thank you, Mr. Shaw," she said.

As Mr. Shaw started to drive away, Annie called, "Thank you for showing me how to load the rifle and how to shoot it!"

Mr. Shaw called back, "You didn't need anybody to show you how to shoot." He shook his head. "I never saw the like!"

Annie waved. Then she turned to the children. They were quiet, watching Old Pink leave home. Annie rang the cowbell. "First I must clean the rifle and put it back. Then let's make up a game!" she said gaily. "Here, Hulda, you stay here and hold the cowbell, and I'll be back in just a few minutes."

In the cabin, she lovingly worked over the gun until it was again shining inside and out. She replaced it on the pegs and ran outside.

"I know! We can take turns being a runaway cow!" Annie suggested.

"Me first! Me first!" Hulda jumped up and down, clanging the bell.

"All right."

Hulda went "Moo-ooo!" She ran around the yard, ringing the bell as hard as she could. "Catch me, catch me!" she screamed joyfully. "I'm a runaway cow!"

Soon they were so out of breath that no one remembered to be sad about Old Pink's going away. Annie didn't even have time to think about how she had just shot Father's gun for the first time in her life.

She even forgot about the quail trap until that afternoon. It was Johnny who reminded her. "Let's go see it," he urged.

The trap was still empty, but this time Annie did not mind so much. She was thinking about Father's rifle.

"There are other ways of getting quail," she said to Johnny. "I'll tell Mother what Mr. Shaw said about the way I handled the gun. Maybe she'll let me go hunting with the rifle now."

When Mother came in that evening she was carrying packages. "Mr. Shaw gave me the money for Old Pink," she said. "He took me into Greenville in his wagon. I bought some things we need. I also bought some surprises for all my children."

The six children gathered around their mother. It had been a long time since they had had surprises from town. There were smooth bars of soap for the three older girls. The girls exclaimed over their sweet-smelling presents. "They're not like the soft brown soap we make ourselves!" they said.

"Is my surprise soap, too?" Johnny asked. He looked disappointed.

Mother laughed and handed him a brown paper sack. "Look and see, child," she said.

Johnny reached into the sack. He pulled out a short, slender stick with something round at one end. The round part was white with red stripes.

"What is it? What is it?" Johnny cried, jumping up and down excitedly.

"I forgot thee hasn't had candy for so long thee doesn't know what it looks like," Mother said. "It's a peppermint sucker, an all-day sucker!" Mother gave Annie and Hulda suckers, too. "Save them until after supper," she said.

Supper was gay that night. The cornmeal mush was good. The homemade bread was spread with fresh, sweet butter.

Annie told Mother about Mr. Shaw. "He was nice," she said. She told how she had been lady of the house and invited her guest to have a cup of tea. "But he was more interested in the rifle," she added. Then she told how Mr. Shaw had showed her how to load the rifle, and how he had let her fire it.

Annie jumped up from her chair, swinging an imaginary gun to her shoulder. She took aim and pretended to bring down a walnut. Then she made the family laugh with her imitation of Mr. Shaw. Like him, she solemnly shook her head. She tried to make her voice deep like his when he said, "I never saw the like! Never in all my life!"

Mother laughed with the rest. "Yes, Mr. Shaw told me how amazed he was at thy skill."

Annie thought, "Now is the time. I'll ask her now, but I won't tell her it's because I want to get something special for her birthday dinner. I'll keep that for a surprise."

Then she said aloud, "You will let me go hunting now, won't you, Mother? I can load the rifle all by myself. Mr. Shaw showed me just how to do it. I could shoot a quail or a rabbit or a squirrel to bring home. I'm sure I could!"

Mother smiled. "Quail and rabbits and squirrels don't stay still like walnuts. Thee might find them harder to hit." Then, growing serious, she went on. "Thee knows I have no love for guns, Annie. If that rifle had not belonged to Father, I would have sold it long ago. I may have to sell it yet. Besides, thee is too young, child. I don't want thee to take a dangerous thing like that in the woods. I would not have thee get hurt. I would not have thee harm any animal unless it's needed for food, either."

"People get hurt only when they don't know how to handle guns, Mother," Annie argued. "I know how. Mr. Shaw said so."

"Perhaps, Annie, but wait till thee is older.

Then we'll see. We have food to eat. It is not necessary for thee to go hunting."

Mother's voice was firm. Annie knew there was no use to beg.

Johnny jumped up from the table. "The candy! It's time for the all-day suckers!"

Annie looked at hers. "It's almost too pretty to eat," she said. "I think I'll save mine for a while."

"Not me!" Johnny was over by the fireplace, already sucking on his candy. Suddenly the sucker slipped from his hand and broke in a hundred splinters on the stone hearth. "Oh, oh! Mine's all smashed!" he cried. "Now I don't have any sucker." His face was sad.

Annie hesitated just a second. Then she ran to her brother. "Here, Tag. You take mine. I haven't even licked it yet."

Johnny cheered up at once. He put as much of Annie's sucker into his mouth as he could.

When he said, "Thank you, Annie," his mouth was so full he could hardly talk.

Mother smiled at Annie. "Sometimes thee is bigger than thee looks, child."

Her mother's words made Annie feel better, but she wished that she looked big, too.

BIRTHDAY DINNER

Every day Annie and Johnny took a secret journey to the trap. The corn lay uneaten in the little trench. It looked as if no animal had even touched it. Johnny was discouraged. So was Annie. The next day was Mother's birthday!

When the important day came and Mother left for work, Annie beckoned to Johnny to follow her. Johnny shook his head.

"No use going to that old trap any more," he said. "We'll never catch a quail that way."

Annie's chin went up. Her eyes flashed. "Well,

I'll go by myself then," she said. "Just to have a look."

Annie whirled around and ran across the yard.

"Wait for me!" Johnny cried. "Wait for me! I'm coming, too!"

Annie slowed down. She smiled. "If we don't find anything today, Tag, you won't have to look any more. Today's the day that's important."

When they reached the little trench, Annie stopped short. "Look, Tag," she whispered. "The corn is gone!"

Annie and Johnny tiptoed toward the brush-covered trap. They listened. Was that a rustling they heard? Annie held her breath as she lifted branches off the trap.

"Oooh!" Annie and Johnny said together.

"Two of them, Tag! Not one quail but two!" Annie was so excited that she turned a handspring. Johnny turned one, too.

They watched the quail for a minute. The

birds fluttered their wings, but the strong little trap held them fast.

"Now we'll have to figure out how to get them home." Annie thought a minute. "I'll lift one corner of the trap, Tag. You reach in and grab one quail by the legs. It will flop around, but you hold tight with both hands. Don't let go. Then I'll grab the other one."

Annie looked at her brother anxiously. "Remember," she said. "We'll have to hold tight, no matter what they do. Do you think you can, Tag? It won't be easy."

Johnny's face was serious. "Yes, I'll hold tight," he said.

"All right then," Annie said. "Let's get down on our hands and knees. I'll count to three, and when I say three I'll lift up this corner of the trap. Then you grab one of the quail. Now! One—two—three!"

Johnny's hands closed around the quail's legs.

The bird flapped its wings wildly. It jerked and pulled, but Johnny held on tight. Then Annie caught the other quail with one hand. With the other hand she pushed over the trap.

"If we can only get them home all right now," Annie panted. Her face was pink. Her eyes were bright with excitement.

"We've done it, Tag! We've done it!" she cried. "Won't Mother be surprised and pleased?"

On the way home Johnny tripped over a stone. He stumbled and nearly fell. His quail almost got away then, but he held tight.

When they came into the yard, Annie began calling. "Lyda, Lyda, come quick! See what we've got! We've got Mother's birthday dinner! Everybody, come look!"

Lyda came to the door, followed by Sarah Ellen, Elizabeth, and little Hulda. What a commotion there was then! Everyone laughed and exclaimed and talked at once.

"It's wonderful!" Sarah Ellen said. "Mother will be so pleased."

Lyda said, "How in the world did you two children do it?"

Annie and Johnny looked at each other and grinned.

"We found a way," Annie said mysteriously.

That night Mother and the whole Moses family had a feast. The quail were plump and tender. Mother roasted them over the hot ashes in the fireplace. Then she put them on the table, along with the rest of the meal, and the family sat down to eat.

When dinner was over, Johnny said, "Quail is even better than all-day suckers."

Everyone agreed.

Mother looked at Annie with a twinkle in her eye. "I never saw the like!" she said, shaking her head as Mr. Shaw had done. "Never in all my life!"

Old Black

ALL THAT YEAR and the next Annie built traps. She caught quail. She trapped grouse, too. The family had all the meat they wanted.

Annie wandered farther and farther away from the cabin to trap her game. She jumped nimbly over the swampy places along the streams. She roamed through the meadows and deep into the woods.

Her mother worried about her. "I wonder if thee will ever be a proper young lady," she said to Annie. "Thee is more at home in the woods than in the cabin. Thee must not grow up like a young wild turkey. Thee is almost nine now.

70

It is time to learn how to be clever with a needle like thy sisters."

So, in the evenings, when the supper table was cleared and the family gathered together, Annie learned to sew. Her needle moved more and more quickly in and out of the cloth.

One night she was seated at the table with her mother and sisters. The soft yellow light of the oil lamp fell on her chestnut hair as she bent her head over her sewing. She was turning up the hem of a skirt that had once belonged to Lyda.

"I remember when I wove that material for Lyda so that she could make a skirt for herself," Mother said.

"That skirt has been a good hand-me-down," Lyda said with a smile. "First it was mine. Then, when it got too small for me, I handed it down to Sarah Ellen."

"I wore it one winter and handed it down to Elizabeth," Sarah Ellen said.

Elizabeth added, "It was my favorite skirt. Now it's much too short for me, so I'm glad to hand it down to Annie."

Annie looked up. "Well, I'm glad I have it. It should fit just right when I get the hem turned up. When I get too big for it, I'll hand it down to Hulda."

"Goody," Hulda said.

Lyda laughed. "If there's anything left of it by that time!" She looked at Annie's sewing with approval. "My, you're making that hem straight, and you don't even use the tape measure! I remember when I made my first hem. It was as crooked as a cowpath!"

With a flourish, Annie took the last few stitches in the hem. She snipped off the thread. She shook out her skirt and slipped it on over her old one. She whirled about. "How does it look?" she asked.

"It fits thee well and looks very nice," Mother

said. "That chestnut brown goes nicely with thy hair. But the best part about it is that thee sewed the hem without help."

Annie beamed. She whirled again. "I didn't know that sewing was so much fun! Fixing a skirt is as much fun as—well, as fixing a corn-stalk trap!"

The girls laughed at this, but Johnny didn't. "I'd rather fix traps any day." He looked anxiously at Annie. "I hope you don't stay indoors all the time now, just to sit around and sew!"

"No, Tag," Annie told him. "I still like to go outdoors, too. Especially now that it's spring again. Today I saw the first Johnny-jump-up in the woods. I think that's my favorite wild flower. You never know what you'll see next this time of year."

The next day, Annie and Johnny were out gathering sassafras bark and roots. Mother wanted some to add to her supply of homemade medicine. They were busy working among the sassafras trees when Annie heard a noise. It was a crashing, lumbering noise in the woods.

"It's an animal of some kind," Johnny said. "Sounds like a bear."

Annie laughed. "Probably just a wild hog. Or somebody's ox that's run away."

The noise grew louder. It sounded much closer. The children peered through the trees.

"Look, there comes your bear!" Annie said.

"Why, it's just a cow, a big black cow," Johnny answered.

The cow ran this way and that. She gave a loud bellow.

"Look out!" Annie said. "She's wild. She doesn't look gentle like Old Pink. Mother told me once that cows act that way sometimes when they've been lost for a few days."

The cow bellowed again. Johnny put his hands over his ears.

74

"I wonder where she came from," Annie went on. "She doesn't look like any cow in our neighborhood. Have you ever seen her?"

Johnny shook his head.

Annie drew him behind a big tree, and the two watched from there. The cow plunged in and out among the trees, mooing.

"Poor Old Black," Annie said. "She can't find her way out. She's just going 'round and 'round in circles."

Finally Annie and Johnny could see that the cow was growing tired. She was going more and more slowly now. Then she stopped in a little clearing and lay down. She mooed softly once and closed her eyes.

"I wish we could take her home," Johnny said. "Then we could have milk every day instead of whenever Mr. Shaw can spare some for us."

"Well, we ought to take her home for tonight, anyhow," Annie said. "We could put her in Old

Pink's stall until we find out where she came from and who owns her."

"How can we get her home if she's so wild?" asked Johnny.

Annie answered, "I don't know, but we can try." The cow seemed gentle enough now that she was asleep. "I know," Annie went on. "I'll go get some grass. She probably hasn't found any in these thick woods."

Annie ran out of the woods into the nearby field. She found some grass, fresh and green. She filled her new skirt with it. Back in the little clearing in the woods, she started quietly toward the cow.

Johnny followed close behind her. "What if she starts after us?" he whispered.

"Just climb the nearest tree," Annie whispered in reply.

Now that Annie was close to the cow, it seemed as big as a mountain to her. She lost some of

her bravery. Did she dare waken the cow? Then she said softly, "Here, Old Black. Here's some supper for you."

Old Black opened her eyes.

Johnny got ready to run. Annie held her skirt in one hand. In the other she held out some of the fresh grass. "Good Old Black," she said. "Good supper."

The cow glared at the children.

Johnny took a step toward the nearest tree, but Annie stood perfectly still.

The cow looked straight at Annie with her big brown eyes. What would she do next? Annie was ready to run. Then the cow opened her mouth and nibbled the grass.

"Nice Old Black," Annie went on in a quiet voice. "Nice Black, you come home with us." Annie started to back out of the clearing, the grass still in her hand.

Old Black lumbered to her feet. She followed

Annie through the trees and took more nibbles from her hand.

Annie was afraid the cow might run away when she led it to the field, but it didn't. Instead, it kept following her as if her gentle, kind voice had a kind of magical effect on it. It followed her meekly and peacefully all the way home and let her tie it up in Old Pink's stall in the shed behind the house.

All the Moses family were delighted. Mother said, "Annie, thee has a way with animals, just as thee has with children. We'll give the cow a good home until we can find her owner. Meantime, Johnny, get the pail for me. The cow wants milking."

"We want the milk, too," said Johnny hungrily.

Annie looked down at herself. "Oh, dear!" she cried. "Look at my nice new skirt! It's covered with grass stains."

"Don't worry about them, Annie," Lyda said.

"I can take them out with a little ammonia. Besides, who cares about a few grass stains when we have a fine big cow like Old Black. I do hope we can keep her, Mother. It would be so nice to have a cow again, and all the milk we can use. I've missed Old Pink."

"So have we!" cried Hulda and Johnny together.

"I would like to keep her, too," Mother said. "However, she must belong to someone, and we can't keep something that belongs to someone else. I will ask around and see what I can learn."

Several days later Mother learned from one of the neighbors that the cow had run away from the farm of a family that had moved west. By this time the family must be far away, but nobody knew where. Even if she tried, there was no way that Mother could find them.

One day Mr. Shaw happened by the cabin, and Annie told him about Old Black.

He listened gravely, then said, "Well, if you can't find the owners, I guess it's finders keepers. You found the cow, and you have as much right to her as anyone else."

"That's good," said Annie. "She found us and we found her. I think I'll give her Old Pink's bell. Then she will seem like a real member of the family."

A Shower
of Sparks

DURING ALL these months, Annie took good care
of the rifle. The next fall, just after she was
nine, she hoped her mother would think she was
old enough to go hunting. Instead, her mother
said, "Not yet. Thee had best stay with the trap-
ping this winter. Perhaps when thee is ten thee
may use the rifle."

The older girls kept the cabin as neat as a
pin. Annie was a big help to her older sisters,
but she still liked to polish the rifle after her
dusting and scrubbing were done. She rubbed
the brass star set in the stock until it glittered
more brightly than a real star. She cleaned out

the long barrel carefully and oiled the trigger and the hammer.

"I just know I could hunt with this rifle," she thought. "If Mother ever decides I am big enough to take it out, I want it to be shining and ready to use."

However, one night early in winter, Mother brought home some bad news. "I may have a chance to sell the rifle," she said. "Mr. La Motte at the store knows a man who wants a good rifle. Mr. La Motte told him about Father's."

Annie cried out in dismay. "Don't sell it! Please don't! It's our treasure."

"Why, child, I know it is valuable," Mother said. "Besides, I value it because it was Father's. But we don't really need it, and we do need money."

Annie looked so sad that Mother added, "I haven't said 'yes' yet. I told Mr. La Motte that I'd have to think it over."

Annie drew a breath of relief. The matter wasn't really settled yet. Maybe Mother would say "no" to the hunter after all.

Still, Annie could not help worrying. She worried that night. She woke up worrying the next day. She thought she couldn't bear it if someone bought the rifle before she had a chance to go hunting with it. "I've shot the rifle only once in my whole life," she thought. "Now maybe I'll never have the chance again."

The next afternoon Lyda's friend Joe Stein came by on his way to Greenville. "Annie, how would you three young'uns like a pet rooster?" he asked.

"All our own? Our very own?" Annie and Johnny cried together.

Hulda clapped her hands.

"Yes," said Joe. "I've got him out in the wagon. Now that winter's coming on and I'm making so many trips to Cincinnati, I can't take care of

84

him. He's yours if you want him. I'll give you some feed for him, too."

"Let's go see him!" Annie ran to the door. Johnny and Hulda were right at her heels. When Annie opened the door, all three of them stopped short in amazement.

"He's coming to see us!" Johnny exclaimed.

There stood the rooster, right on the doorstep. He cocked his head and looked at the children sharply with bright eyes. His red comb stood up like a flag. His glossy black tail feathers curved high and handsome.

"Pretty rooster," Hulda called.

Then everyone laughed because the rooster walked right into the cabin as though he belonged there.

Joe said, "He follows me around. He will follow you around, too, when he gets to know you."

"What's his name?" asked Annie, as she stroked his glossy feathers.

"I call him Trumpet," Joe answered.

"Trumpet?" Hulda asked. "Why do you call him that?"

Joe laughed. "You'll find out early tomorrow morning when he wakes you up." Then he turned to Lyda. "Would any of you young ladies like to drive into town with me?"

Lyda was delighted. Her cheeks were pink as she untied her apron. Sarah Ellen and Elizabeth were pleased, too. They did not often have the chance to ride into town. There were signs of snow in the sky, and the family might be snowbound before long.

Lyda said, "Annie, you can take care of things here, can't you? See that Johnny chops some wood for the fire. Please wash the dishes, and look after Hulda, too."

"We'll all take care of Trumpet while you're gone," Hulda said.

"All right," Lyda said with a laugh. "Take him

outside, though. No rooster belongs in the house, not even a pet."

When the big girls had bundled up and gone, the children ran outside. At once Trumpet strutted out after them.

Johnny said, "Where will he sleep at night if Lyda won't let him stay in the house?"

"He can roost in the rafters above Old Black's stall," Annie said. "It would be a good idea to make him a coop sometime this winter. Winter is when hungry varmints come 'round."

"What's a varmint?" Hulda asked.

"Oh, any animal that's up to no good," Annie explained. "Foxes, wolves maybe, wildcats, weasels, and such. We wouldn't want any of them to get Trumpet."

"Bad varmints," Hulda said.

Johnny looked at Trumpet thoughtfully. "Wish I didn't have to chop wood. I could start making a coop today."

"Well, chores come first," Annie said. "I'll wash dishes now. Hulda, you can play out here with the rooster. Just don't leave the yard."

"I won't," Hulda promised.

Everything was peaceful for a while. Annie could hear Johnny's hatchet as he split kindling. She could hear Hulda talking to the rooster.

Suddenly Johnny burst into the house. "A varmint!" he cried. "I saw a fox. He'll get Trumpet! What'll we do?"

Annie said, "Get Hulda and the rooster in here fast." She ran to the fireplace. She climbed up on the bench and lifted the gun down.

Quickly she did what she had watched Mr. Shaw do. She took the stopper out of the powder horn and shook some powder into her hand. "I hope that's not too much," she said to herself. Cupping her hand over the muzzle, she shook the powder down into the long barrel. She spilled a little on the hearth, but she did not notice that.

By now Johnny and Hulda and the rooster were all in the kitchen. "Are you sure it was a fox?" Annie asked.

"He was reddish," Johnny said excitedly. "He had a bushy tail."

"That sounds like a fox." Annie hurried with her loading. She pushed the patch and ball down with the ramrod. Quickly she pulled back the hammer and put the percussion cap in place.

"You all stay in here," she told the children. "You can watch out the window. I'll see if I can get that varmint."

Outside, Annie looked first at Old Black in the shed. The cow was quiet. Then Annie looked out over the field. There were a few flakes of snow in the air, but no fox was in sight.

Annie stood perfectly still, waiting. Then she heard a noise. It was in the bushes beside the fence. She listened. Yes, there it was again, a quiet rustling sound. Annie raised the rifle to her shoulder. She aimed at the spot where she heard the noise and pulled the trigger.

There was a sharp *bang!* The gun jerked. The stock jumped up and hit her in the face.

"Ooh!" she cried in pain, putting her hand quickly to her nose.

A shrill, frightened yelp came from behind the fence, and a reddish-brown dog sprang out and ran yelping across the field.

Johnny rushed out from the house followed by Hulda and Trumpet. "Did you get the fox?"

Annie pointed to the stray dog, running across the field. "There goes your fox! How awful if I had hit the dog! It was lucky for him that I couldn't see him!"

Johnny looked at her face. "Your nose is all red. It's swelling."

"Yes, but I don't care," Annie said. "This has taught me never to aim at a noise. That's a rule I'll never forget."

"Does your nose hurt, Annie?" Johnny asked anxiously. "It looks bad."

"Yes, it does," Annie replied. "I won't put so much powder in the next time. That's what made the rifle kick."

"Mother won't let you try again. She says you're not big enough to shoot a gun."

"I know," Annie admitted. "I didn't think about that. I didn't think about anything except that a fox might be prowling around the cabin. I didn't want him to scare Hulda or run off with Trumpet. But all that happened was that I nearly hurt a dog and did hurt my face."

"Do you think we'll get a scolding?" Johnny asked anxiously. "It was partly my fault."

Annie thought a minute. "Well, since everything turned out all right, let's not say anything about it. If Mother asks any questions, I'll tell her everything. Don't worry, Tag. I'll take the scolding if there is one."

Then it began to snow hard. Johnny chopped more wood. Annie cleaned the rifle, then carried armloads of wood into the kitchen. Hulda played with Trumpet in the falling snow. He ruffled his feathers and cocked his head.

Mother came home early because of the snow. She did not ask any questions. She laughed at Trumpet's antics. She agreed that he made a fine pet. "He can roost in Old Black's stall," she said. "He will be out of the wet weather there, and he won't bother us here in the house."

Once or twice she looked curiously at Annie's nose. But she said nothing about it. Once in the house she asked about the other girls. Then she put the kettle on to make a cup of spicewood tea. She started to brush up the hearth. Suddenly the gunpowder Annie had spilled began to spark. When it was brushed into the fire, a shower of sparks flew upward.

Mrs. Moses looked at the bright sparks. She looked at the rifle above the fireplace. Then she looked gravely at Annie.

Annie's heart was pounding. She took a deep breath. "I loaded the gun and fired it, Mother," she confessed.

"I see," her mother said quietly. "Why did thee fire the gun?"

Annie told her mother all about it. When Annie finished, Mother was silent for a minute.

She looked so serious that Annie was sure she would be punished.

Finally her mother said, "It is good to know thee is big enough now to guard the children when the three of you are left alone. Thee did right to act quickly when thee thought there was danger, Annie. Still, it would have been a sad thing if thee had shot the dog. Before thee fires the rifle next time, thee must make very sure the danger is real."

"Next time?" Annie asked eagerly. "You mean you're not going to punish me?"

Her mother smiled. "I think thee has been punished enough. Come, let me put some butter on thy poor nose. It is as red as a love apple." The butter was cool and soothing. "There! Now let's start supper for the girls."

As Annie helped her mother, her heart was light, but it sank when her sisters came home with a message. They came in stamping the snow off their feet and shaking it off their coats. Their cheeks and noses were pink with cold.

"Mr. La Motte wants us to tell you that a hunter is coming to look at the rifle in a day or two," Lyda said to Mother. "He has his heart set on buying it. He's ready to pay a good price if it's as fine a gun as he hears it is."

Annie looked quickly at her mother. "Don't let him come," she begged.

Mother answered quietly, "No harm in his looking. Perhaps he won't think it so fine after all."

Annie knew that he would. She looked at the long gun, shining in the firelight. Surely it was the best rifle in all of Ohio!

A Real Wolf

THAT NIGHT Annie lay awake. Everything was quiet. The only thing she could hear was the hissing of the kitchen fire. The wet snow must be spitting down the chimney on the hot coals.

Annie snuggled deeper into the soft feather bed. "I hope it snows and snows and snows," she thought. "I hope the snow piles clear up to the rooftop. Then nobody, not even a hunter, can come to see us." She sighed contentedly.

She was drifting off to sleep when something made her stiffen. What was that? She listened. There it came again from far away—a long low howl. "A wolf!" she thought. "Nothing but a wolf howls like that." Annie felt a prickle of fear. "The wolves are out tonight."

Again the long howl came. Was it nearer this time? "Of course, Mother says wolves don't attack people," Annie reminded herself. "That is, hardly ever. Just the same, she has always warned us to keep out of their way. In the winter when food is hard to find they grow hungry." Annie shivered. "I'm glad Trumpet is up on a rafter in the shed."

Annie was glad, too, that there was a strong bar across the kitchen door. They were snug and safe in the cabin. Annie fell asleep. The snow kept falling, soft and thick. It snowed all night.

At the first crack of daylight, the whole family was awakened by a loud, joyful "cock-a-doodle-doo!" Annie wondered sleepily who was blowing a horn. Again came the trumpeting. This time it was louder and longer. "Cock-a-doodle-doo-oo-oo!"

Annie sat up in bed. "It's Trumpet. I forgot all about him."

Johnny asked, "Is it time to get up?"

"Not yet," Mother murmured. "Go back to sleep. We don't have to get up with the rooster."

Once more there was the joyful sound of the rooster. "Cock-a-doodle-doo-oo-oo!"

Lyda laughed softly. "Now you know why Joe called him Trumpet. His horn blows everyone awake."

The window panes were gray with pale morning light. It really was too early to get up. At last Trumpet stopped crowing. Everybody went back to sleep.

When Annie next opened her eyes, the room was full of light. She ran to the window. "Look, look!" she cried happily. "Everything is white. The whole world is white!"

The trees bent low under their burden of white. The snow had drifted into huge mounds.

They weren't as high as the roof, but drifts had piled up around the walls of the cabin. They had blown into Old Black's shed. The snow was so high that Annie couldn't even see the rail fence. It was buried under a woolly blanket.

The sun came out. Everything glittered. "It looks as if all the stars have fallen. See how they sparkle in the snow," Annie said.

Mother was gay, too. "It's a real holiday. I won't even try to go out. I couldn't get very far if I did. It's a good thing my patient was much better yesterday. She won't need me today."

Annie and Johnny dug a path to the shed so they could milk Old Black and feed the rooster. They took turns with the shovel, tossing snow into the air. They made walls as high as their heads on either side of the path. When they came in with their pail of milk, their noses were red from the cold.

"Old Black wouldn't stand still," Annie said.

"Tag had to hold her so I could do the milking. She's excited by the snow, too, and Trumpet is mad at it. When we fed him he kept pulling up one foot and standing on the other."

That afternoon Johnny and Annie had a snowball fight. Johnny's aim was good, but Annie's aim was better. She forced Johnny to retreat behind Old Black's shed.

Finally Johnny poked his head around to see if it were safe to come out. He pulled back just in time. Annie's last snowball whizzed past. Johnny peeked out again. Annie bent over to make more ammunition. Johnny rushed out. Before Annie could turn, he stuffed snow down her neck.

Annie shrieked and grabbed her brother. They fell into the snow together and rolled over and over like two bear cubs. Trumpet fluttered around and hopped after them.

When they picked themselves up and went

into the house, Johnny said, "I won't have to wash my face for supper tonight, Mother. Annie's washed it with snow already."

Supper over, the children cracked nuts by the hearth. Mother, near the fire, darned long wool stockings. Sometimes she hummed a tune. Then the rest would join in.

"How cozy it is tonight by the fire," Lyda murmured. "I like nights like this."

Just then Old Black mooed.

Annie frowned. "What's the matter with her? She's usually sound asleep by now."

The cow mooed again, louder.

Mother stopped her darning and listened. "Could something be wrong?"

Lyda answered. "Maybe she can't get to sleep with all this snow. She isn't used to it. But she does sound strange."

Suddenly Old Black bellowed and Trumpet squawked loudly.

Annie jumped to her feet. "She's scared! Something is the matter! I'll go see!"

Johnny dashed to the door after her.

"Do be careful," Mother called. Mother and the older girls crowded around the door. Annie and Johnny stopped and listened. They all peered out into the night. The moon was up. It made a blue path along the snow-covered ground by the shed.

Annie's keen eyes caught sight of an animal running behind the shed. This time it was no dog. Without a word Annie whirled back into the kitchen. She ran for the gun.

The animals in the shed knew there was danger nearby. Old Black mooed again. Trumpet squawked. He flopped around among the rafters. Johnny started toward the shed.

At the same instant something large and gray and furry darted out from behind the shed and went straight to the open door.

"A wolf!" Lyda cried. "It's a wolf!"

Mother gasped, "Johnny, look out!"

The group in the doorway froze with fear.

Then everything happened at once. Annie ran out to the doorstep and swung the loaded rifle to her shoulder.

Johnny got in the way of the wolf, which lunged against him, knocking the breath out of him. Johnny went down like a sack of meal. The wolf turned and ran from the shed.

A shot rang out, and the wolf fell to the ground. Inside the shed, Old Black kicked against her stall. Trumpet squawked and fluttered on his rafter.

Mother, Annie, and the others ran to the boy on the ground. "Johnny! Johnny!"

Annie was the first to reach him. Then everyone crowded around the boy. By this time Old Black was bellowing and kicking frantically.

"Oh, Johnny!" cried Mother, bending over him. "Is thee killed?"

Johnny opened his eyes. "I—I don't think so," he gasped. "There was a wolf! Where did he go? What happened?" He got to his feet slowly and looked around.

"There he is," said Annie, pointing. There on the snow, a little distance away, lay the dead wolf. It looked even bigger now than it had when it was alive.

The older girls began to pet Old Black until

she was calm again. Hulda coaxed Trumpet down from his roost.

"Trumpet, nice Trumpet," she crooned, stroking his feathers. "The wolf is all gone. Annie dead-ed him."

"Yes, and tomorrow we'd better skin him," Lyda said. "Wolf pelts are valuable. Does anybody know how to skin a wolf?"

Mother laughed a shaky little laugh. "We've skinned rabbits. I guess we can skin a wolf if we have to."

Then she turned to Annie. Her eyes were tender as she looked at her small daughter. "Tonight thee knew a real danger when thee saw one. Thee is a big girl, Annie, bigger than I realized."

The love and pride in her voice made Annie feel a foot taller.

Hulda tugged at her mother's skirt. "Trumpet wants to sleep in our house tonight. Please let him, Mother."

"If thee wishes, yes. Just for tonight, though, because if there is any more danger, Annie will take care of it with her gun."

"My gun?" Annie asked eagerly.

Mother smiled. "Yes. From now on the gun belongs to Annie to do with as she wishes."

Annie hugged her mother hard. Then she grabbed Johnny around the waist and whirled him around until they were both dizzy.

Mother laughed. "And I thought thee was so grown up," she said to Annie.

At that Annie stopped whirling, smoothed back her hair and walked quietly toward the house. She paused at the doorstep where she had left her rifle. She stooped to pick it up. "It's my gun," she said quietly, almost to herself. "I still can't believe it!"

The rest of the family followed her into the house. Last of all came Trumpet. He swaggered after them.

"Just look at him," Lyda said. "He's not afraid of any old wolf, at least not a dead one."

The next day the hunter who wanted to buy the rifle came. He rode his horse through the snow up to the door of the cabin. Mother met him at the door.

"Thee is welcome to come in and visit, but the rifle is not for sale," she said.

The hunter looked puzzled. "La Motte said you didn't need your rifle," he said. "He said you didn't have a hunter on the place."

"Yes, that's what I thought," Mother answered. "I was mistaken. We have an expert hunter here, and the rifle is hers. I'm sorry, but Annie's gun is not for sale." Then she added, "Not at any price. Now would thee like a cup of tea?"

Annie Leaves Home

ONE DAY Annie and Johnny slipped quietly into Frenchy La Motte's shop. Johnny set a bundle down on the counter. The two children waited in silence.

The shop was full of shadows. A stove in one corner glowed red hot. Around it were a half dozen men warming their hands and feet. They were trappers, come to swap stories. No one noticed the two small figures by the counter.

As the children's eyes became more used to the dimness, they looked around them. They saw animal skins piled high along the walls—raccoon, muskrat, and mink. There were even a few

108

deer hides. The counter was loaded with boxes of knives, lanterns, packages of gun powder— all kinds of hunting supplies. Traps were stacked on the floor.

"Real traps," Annie whispered. "Not like our cornstalk traps." Johnny nodded.

On the wall over the counter a few guns gleamed in their racks. Annie looked at the guns with wide eyes. She nudged Johnny. "They look good, but not so good as my rifle."

Johnny nodded again. He was overcome at the sight of so many fine things.

They listened to the end of a long story one of the trappers was telling. "Yes, sir," he finished. "There's nothing quite so tricky as a wild turkey. They're smart critters. I tracked one gobbler all day. In the end he got away."

There was silence for a minute. Annie wished Mr. La Motte would come to wait on them. She could see his red beard glowing in the light from the stove. Finally she coughed softly to attract his attention.

The men looked up. Frenchy La Motte got out of his chair and came toward them. He was quick and lively. "Like a robin," Annie thought.

"I'm sorry," he said. "I didn't know I had customers. What can I do for you young ones?"

Annie pointed to their bundle. "Would you look at that, please?" she asked.

Mr. La Motte unwrapped the package and gave a low whistle. "A wolf skin!" he exclaimed. "It's a beauty, too, and heavy. Dark gray fur from the back and pale fur from the belly." He looked sharply at Annie and Johnny. "Where'd you two get it?"

Now the men came to crowd around. They fingered the fur. They exclaimed over its thickness and odor.

Annie kept her eyes on Mr. La Motte. "We got it out at our place, Mrs. Moses' cabin," she said.

"The wolf got in our shed. It was probably after our pet rooster."

"Who shot him?" Mr. La Motte asked.

Johnny jerked his thumb toward Annie. "She did," he said.

Annie nodded.

The men looked at the little girl. They could not believe it. They shook their heads.

Johnny spoke up. "Honest she did. Tell them how you did it, Annie."

Annie felt shy. She looked at Mr. La Motte.

"We're all hunters and trappers here," he said. "We like to swap stories. Now it's your turn, little lady. Tell us just what happened. Begin at the beginning."

Annie looked around at the small group of men. They seemed friendly but doubtful. "They really don't believe us," she thought.

"Go on, Annie, show them," Johnny urged.

Annie could tell that Johnny was counting on

her to prove herself and her story. He looked spunky. She mustn't disappoint him. She began to feel spunky herself. Her chin went up. Her gray eyes snapped.

"We were all sitting around our fireplace one snowy night," she began in her sweet voice. "Suddenly our cow began to bellow."

As she went on, Annie began to warm to her story. She couldn't keep her feet still. When she came to the part about going out to the doorstep, she ran over to the window and peered out. Step by step she acted out what had happened. She ran back to the wall counter and took down the gun from the lowest rack. She checked it to make sure it was empty, then pretended to load it.

The men watched in amazement. Here was a little girl, not even ten years old, who handled the long heavy rifle like an old-timer. Her small hands were clever and quick, and strong, too.

112

When Annie ran lightly over to the window again, she swung the rifle to her shoulder as if she had done it all her life.

"I got back to the step just in time," she went on with her story. "There was the wolf, knocking into Tag and going after our rooster."

She held the gun steady, took aim, and pretended to fire. "Bang!" she cried.

"You got him!" Johnny shouted.

"I believe you did, young lady, I believe you did," said Mr. La Motte. "I can tell by the way you handled that gun!" He went over to Annie and shook her hand.

The men stirred and nodded. One of them said, "Well, if any girl could shoot a wolf, I believe this one could." The others agreed.

Frenchy La Motte's red beard bobbed up and down. He waved his hands in the air. "Did you save the ears?" he asked.

Johnny dug deep in a pocket. He pulled out

two pointed, furry, gray ears and handed them to Mr. La Motte. "Here they are."

Mr. La Motte's beard bobbed in approval. "I can get you money for these," he said. "Ohio will pay you a bounty. The state will be glad to be rid of one more wolf. Now, Miss Mozee, what do you want for the pelt?"

Annie looked startled. No one had ever called her "Miss" before. Nobody had ever pronounced "Moses" that way before, either. That must be the French way to say it. Annie liked it. "Miss Mozee," she repeated to herself.

When Annie and her brother left the shop, they carried several things with them. Mother had said they could get whatever they needed. They had gun powder, shot, and percussion caps. They had two sharp hunting knives. They carried a lantern filled with oil. There was more, too, but they would have to come back for it later. Now they had all that they could carry. Best of all, they were to get bounty money from the state for having killed the wolf.

"That will be for Mother," Annie said. "I already have what I want most of all—Father's rifle for my very own to take hunting."

No other wolf appeared at the Moses place after that. All the rest of the winter Annie roamed the fields and woods with her rifle. She brought down all sorts of small game.

Before spring there was a sudden end to her hunting, however. Her mother found a new job.

For a long time Mrs. Moses had not had work. No neighbor had needed her to come and nurse. Money was scarce again. Then, when she was most discouraged, something happened.

Mother smiled as she told her children about it. "I have been made a District Nurse," she said. "That means I'll have regular work. The trouble is that I won't always be able to come home at night. I'll have to stay in some places a long time, and won't be able to be here with my family."

A shadow came into her eyes as she looked around the supper table. "I have thought it all out carefully. Lyda, thee and Sarah Ellen and Elizabeth will stay here to look after the cabin. But my youngest ones" — she looked fondly at her three smallest — "thee will go to stay with friends and neighbors. They have offered kindly to take thee in."

Hulda was excited at the idea of going visiting. She was to stay with the Bartholomews. "Oh, they're nice!" she cried. "They always have candy at their house."

Johnny was to stay with a neighbor who lived nearby. He did not mind. "I can run home often," he said.

Annie's face was sad. "I don't want to go anywhere," she thought. "I want to stay right here in the cabin near the woods."

Her mother saw how Annie felt. "My dear friend, Mrs. Eddington, wants thee, Annie. She is kind and good. She needs thy help. She and her husband are in charge of the big County Home. That is where elderly people and orphan children find a happy home."

"I'm not an orphan!" Annie cried. "I already have a happy home. Besides, the Eddingtons live so far away!"

Mother came over and put her hand gently on Annie's head. "This will always be thy real home, Annie. I pray we will all be here together again before long. But while I have to be away, it will help me to know thee is in Mrs. Eddington's care. She wants thee to take care of her baby."

Annie brightened at the thought of a baby to look after.

Her mother went on, "The real reason I want thee to go is this: They say thee can go to school there. The schoolhouse isn't far from the Home. The Eddingtons will pay for thy books."

Annie jumped up and hugged her mother. "School! I've always wanted to go to school. I can learn to read and write." She looked eagerly at her mother. "Maybe I can even write a letter to you someday."

"Of course thee can, and I'll write to thee as soon as thee learns to read a letter."

A Funny Name

IN NO TIME AT ALL Annie was settled happily at the County Home. She liked the Eddingtons. Mrs. Eddington grew fond of her little visitor. She said she had never seen a child so quick and helpful as Annie.

The Eddingtons had a lot of work to do. They had to look after a big house full of youngsters and elderly people. Annie helped in many ways. By the end of the first week Mrs. Eddington said, "You are like one of my own family. I feel like an auntie with a favorite niece."

Annie called Mrs. Eddington "Auntie." The baby loved Annie, too. He cooed and kicked with joy whenever Annie picked him up from his crib.

The next Monday morning Annie started off to school with the other children from the Home. There were just six weeks of school left, but Annie hoped she could learn fast. She was so excited she almost burst. She skipped along the way to school with the other girls.

When she arrived, all the girls in the schoolyard stopped playing. They gathered around the new girl slowly. At first they just stared at Annie. Then they began to ask questions.

"How old are you?"

Annie gave them a friendly smile. "I'm nine, going-on-ten."

"So'm I," said a girl with yellow curls. She smiled back at Annie shyly.

A tall red-haired girl tossed her head and spoke to Annie. "You don't look going-on-ten. You don't look bigger than seven."

"Well, I'm getting bigger all the time. That's what my mother says, anyhow."

"If you have a mother why are you at the Home?" another tall girl asked. She stood beside the redhead.

"Because my mother is a friend of Mrs. Eddington. I'm visiting there and helping her."

"My name is Kate," said the curly-head. "What's yours?"

"Annie."

"Annie what?"

"Annie Moses."

"That's a funny name," said the tall girl.

"I don't think so," Annie answered.

" 'Tis, too, a funny name," the redhead said. "Moses, Moses, Annie's name is Moses!" she chanted.

Before Annie knew what was happening, the two big girls made a ring. Holding hands, they danced around her. In shrill voices they

chanted, "Moses-Poses! Moses-Noses! Moses-Dozes! Moses-Toses! Annie's name is Moses!"

Annie said nothing. Her cheeks were red, her eyes were bright. She stood as tall as she could, holding her head high.

Before the other girls could get together to rescue her, the school bell rang. The two big girls dashed indoors. Annie and the others followed slowly. "I thought going to school would be fun," she thought. "Now I'm not so sure."

Just then Kate came up and slipped her hand in Annie's. "I like your name," she said. "Don't let those big girls bother you. They always tease new girls at first." Annie smiled gratefully.

The teacher was kind to Annie. She let Annie share a seat with one of the girls from the Home. She brought her a copybook. "Write your name on the cover."

Annie blushed. "I can't write yet," she said in a low voice. A titter came from the seat behind hers where the redhead sat.

"Never mind," the teacher said gently. "I'll write it for you. Then you can copy it. Copy it over and over." The teacher wrote *Annie Moses,* then went back to her desk.

"Moses-Poses!" the tall girl whispered loudly. "Moses-Poses!"

Annie pretended she did not hear. She bent over the paper book. Carefully she tried to copy the teacher's beautiful writing. It was hard to do. "I can hold my rifle still," she thought. "I can make it do anything I want to, but I can't hold my hand still. I can't make the pencil go the right way at all. The letters are all shaky."

She kept on trying. By the end of the morning she was doing better. Just before the bell rang she had written her name so the letters weren't nearly so crooked. She looked at them in wonder. "The letters say *Annie Moses*," she said to herself. "That means me." She sighed. "I never knew anybody before who thought it was a funny name. When I grow up I'm going to change my name. I'll choose a pretty one that everyone will like."

Outdoors after lunch, the red-haired girl and

one of the big boys started choosing sides for games. The redhead chose the other big girl for her side. The boy looked at Annie and grinned in a friendly way.

"Can you run fast?" he asked.

"I'll try hard," Annie said.

"All right. Then I choose you for my team."

When both sides were chosen and the first game of Run-Sheep-Run started, the boy realized how lucky he was to have Annie on his team. Annie ran faster than she had ever run before. She ran faster than all the girls and faster than most of the boys. She was the first one to touch home base.

The boys and girls on her side were delighted. At the end of the game they shouted, "We won! We won because Annie was on our side!"

For the second game, the red-haired girl said, "This time I want Annie on my team."

"No, she's staying on our team, aren't you,

Annie?" one boy said. "Anyhow, it's my turn to choose first, and I choose Annie."

Back at the Home, Annie said to Mrs. Eddington, "School is going to be fun. Today I made lots of new friends, and already I know how to write my name. At first there were two big girls who teased me about my name, but I pretended I didn't care. After recess they didn't bother me any more."

"I'm proud of you, Annie," Mrs. Eddington said. "I like your spunk."

The days went fast. School was over in a few weeks. "I still can't write much," Annie said. "Not enough to write a letter to Mother."

"Never mind," Auntie answered. "I'll write for you. I'll tell her that you have decided to stay on and go to school next fall."

Annie didn't stay, however. One hot July day a stranger came to the Home and changed all of Annie's plans.

He drove up to the Home in a fine carriage. He had dinner with the Eddingtons. Annie listened as he talked about his big farm, miles away. He smiled at Annie.

"He seems nice, but there's something I don't like about his smile," Annie thought. "He smiles as if he doesn't really mean it."

He turned to Annie. "How old are you?"

"I'll be ten next month."

Auntie spoke up. "Annie does everything better than most twelve-year-olds."

"Then she's just the girl I'm looking for," he said. "My wife needs someone to come and help her with our new baby."

"Oh, Annie is just visiting here," Auntie objected. "You can choose one of the other girls. I'd like to put one of them in a nice home. Annie already has a home."

The visitor had made up his mind, however. He wanted Annie. "She looks like a willing worker," he said. He talked about the fine life Annie could have on his farm. There wouldn't be any heavy work for her. She could go to school there, too. "I'll pay her fifty cents a week," the man said at last.

Annie was delighted by this. She had never earned any money. "I don't want it for myself, but would you send it to my mother?" she said.

"I will if you want me to," the man promised.

Auntie Eddington still hesitated. Finally she said, "I don't want to stand in Annie's way. I can't afford to pay her anything myself, and a small, private home would be nice for her. It would be better than this big house where she works so hard. But I'll have to write to her mother and see what she says."

The man promised to come back for Annie. When he had gone, Annie said, "He was nice, but what's wrong with his smile?"

"Why, nothing that I could see," Auntie said.

"Maybe it's because he smiles too much," Annie said. "I don't know."

"Nonsense," Auntie said. "He seemed very nice. Now I'll write to your mother."

Annie's mother answered right away. "Thee says the gentleman seems kind and his wife needs Annie's help," she wrote. "If they give my daughter a happy home and schooling until I send for her, I will be satisfied."

The Runaway

ANNIE SOON FOUND that her new home was anything but happy. After a few days had passed the farmer stopped being kind. He stopped smiling. His wife was always cross, too. Annie wished she could leave. "If only I could write Mother a letter!" she thought.

Annie was not allowed to go to school, however. It was the farmer who wrote to Annie's mother. He did not tell the truth. He said that Annie was so happy and busy that she did not want to go home.

The months dragged on. The only thing that comforted Annie was the thought of the money the farmer was sending home. At least she was helping her mother that way. But why didn't her mother write to her? Annie could not understand why she never got a letter from home.

Then one day in the spring Annie made a discovery. She heard the farmer talking to his wife. "Of course I'm not going to read Annie her mother's letters," he said. "I never even tell her when she gets one. Stop telling me I should send the money to Annie's mother, too. I haven't sent her any money, and I'm not going to. But don't tell the child. She'll work hard as long as she thinks she's helping her mother."

Annie was stunned. All her work had been for nothing! She made up her mind to run away. It would not be easy, for she was more than forty miles from home. Maybe she could take the train. If not, she would walk. She would walk every inch of the way. She would go the first chance she found.

The very next morning Annie was ironing a big basket of sheets. The farmer's wife came out to the kitchen. She put on her bonnet and said, "We're taking the baby and going on business to another farm. We'll be gone all day. You stay at your work. We'll be hungry when we get home, so have supper ready. If I find you haven't done everything, I'll make you sorry."

Annie's heart beat fast. This was her chance. She did not dare look up. The woman might see how excited she was. She just nodded her head and kept the iron moving back and forth over the sheet on the ironing board.

The farmer's wife hurried out. Annie kept on ironing. She listened. At last she heard the wheels of the carriage roll off toward the gate. Carefully she carried the heavy iron over to the stove and set it down. She flew to the front window. There went the carriage up the road!

Annie pressed her face against the window to

watch them leave. "When you get back tonight," she said out loud, "you won't find supper ready. You won't make me sorry, either, because I won't be here. I won't be sorry. I'll be glad!"

Annie ran up to her attic room. Quickly she gathered together her few belongings. She tied string around them to make them into a small bundle, then hurried out.

In no time at all she was out on the road. She turned toward town. The carriage had gone in the opposite direction. Not once did she look back at the house. "I hope I never see it again!" she thought.

Annie took a deep breath. At last she was free! How good the soft breeze felt! How sweetly the birds sang! Her step was light. She saw a meadow lark skimming over a field.

"I wish I had wings," she thought. "If I had wings and could fly home, forty miles would be easy. If I could ride home on the train, though,

134

it would be almost as good as flying. I'd get there almost as soon."

Annie wondered about getting on the train. She had no money. "Perhaps they will let me ride free if I tell them why I am running away. If they won't let me ride, I'll walk all the way home and never get tired." Annie skipped a step or two. Nothing could stop her now. She was on her way home.

It was only a few miles to town. The train didn't leave until afternoon, so she still had time.

When Annie finally reached the little station, she was much too early for the train. There was no one around. She did not want to go indoors. She had been inside enough. She sat down on a wooden bench outside the station. Her feet did not reach the ground. She swung them back and forth. She shaded her eyes and looked down the tracks. They glistened in the sunlight.

"They shine like the barrel of my rifle," she

thought. "The train will come along those tracks, the train that will take me home!"

The bright light on the rails made her feel sleepy. She was tired. She closed her eyes.

Suddenly a voice beside her said, "Going traveling, young lady?"

Annie looked up, startled. An old gentleman was sitting beside her. He was smiling as he looked down at her. His blue eyes were friendly. It had been a long time since Annie had seen such a kind face.

"You look like my granddaughter," he said. "She's coming on the train to visit me. I've come to meet her. Are you going on the train?"

Annie smiled. "I hope so, but I haven't any money to buy a ticket."

The old man looked at her gravely. "You're not running away from home, are you?"

"Oh, no, I've been away," Annie said. "Now I'm trying to go home."

"You'd better tell me all about it," the old man said gently.

Annie told him everything. Her words spilled out as though they had been bottled up inside her for a long time. Finally Annie told how she had run off that morning. "You don't think it was wrong, do you?" she finished anxiously.

"Wrong!" he exploded. "It was the right thing to do! The only thing to do."

A train whistle sounded far down the tracks. Without another word the man got up from the bench. He stomped into the station. When he came back, he had a ticket in his hand.

"Here," he said. "I never bought anything that gave me so much pleasure. I'll tell the conductor to look after you."

When the train came, Annie was put aboard and the conductor was instructed to take care of her.

Late that afternoon Annie jumped off the high

train step at her own station. It was dusk by the time she reached the woods near her mother's cabin. As she hurried along, in and out among the well-known trees, it seemed to her that she had never been away.

Out of the woods, she hurried over the swampy place, across the stream, and through the meadow. Now she could see the cabin. A thread of smoke curled from the chimney. Yellow lamplight spilled out the window.

Annie was so excited she wanted to cry. "If only Mother is there!" she thought. She began to run. She ran in through the opening of the rail fence, on through the yard. She dropped her bundle on the doorstep. She pounded on the door of the cabin.

"Mother! Mother!" she cried.

The door opened. There stood her mother. Annie could not say a word, for her mother's arms were around her, holding her tight.

Homecoming

EVERYONE WAS HAPPY to see Annie. Everybody talked at once. Such a hubbub!

Home was just the same in some ways. In others it was different. Annie was surprised to see Mr. Shaw. He greeted her warmly in his deep voice. He and Mother had been married while Annie was gone.

Annie was delighted, but she looked so surprised that Mother said, "I wrote thee all about the wedding. Didn't the farmer tell thee? That was the time when I told the farmer to send thee home as soon as thee wanted to come."

Annie shook her head. She couldn't bear to

talk about those people. She smiled at Mr. Shaw. She had always liked him.

"We call him Grandpap Shaw," Johnny told Annie fondly.

Annie looked at Johnny and shook her head. "How tall you are, Tag!"

"You seem different, too, Annie—not taller, but more grown-up, maybe," he said.

Hulda hovered near Annie's chair as if she could not get close enough to her sister. But Mother said, "Hulda, it's time for thee to help me put supper on the table. Annie must be hungry."

"Where is Lyda?" Annie asked. "And Sarah Ellen and Elizabeth?"

Mother was surprised. "Surely thee knows they are all married and gone off to homes of their own? Lyda and Joe live in Cincinnati."

Annie found it hard to believe so many things had happened in the months she had been away.

Her mother went on. "Does thee mean to say

141

the farmer never read thee my letters? Was he not telling the truth when he wrote me how happy thee was?"

Annie knew the time had come to tell her mother all about her unhappy stay with the farmer's family. She told it quietly, from beginning to end. Mother and the others listened as though they were hearing about a bad dream.

When Annie finished, her mother's eyes were dark with pain. "To think," she murmured, "all that time I believed them when they wrote me thee was content to stay there. I can never forgive myself."

Annie went to her mother to comfort her. "That's all over and done with," she said cheerfully. "I'm home again now and I'm happy, and that's all that matters."

Mother said, "Thee will not leave home again, child. Not ever, unless thee wants to."

"You can ride the new ponies, too," Hulda said.

"Grandpap Shaw bought them for us, and they're lots of fun."

"I'll teach you how to ride," Johnny said.

Annie smiled. "Do you want to give me shooting lessons, too?" she teased.

Johnny laughed and shook his head. "I've kept the gun polished for you. I've used it, too, but I'll never be as good a shot as you are. Or as good as Grandpap Shaw."

"I'm not the shot I used to be," Mr. Shaw said. "My eyes aren't so good as they used to be."

There was a funny scratching at the door. "What's that?" Annie asked.

Without answering, Hulda ran to open the door. In strutted Trumpet. He cocked his head, ruffled his feathers, then swaggered over to peck at Annie's shoes. Annie leaned over to pet him.

"At least Trumpet hasn't changed, has he?" she said.

"No," said Hulda. "When you hear him in the

143

morning, you'll know for sure that he's just the same!"

The spring and early summer that followed her homecoming were full of fun for Annie. "If only I could see Lyda and the other girls, everything would be perfect," she said one evening.

Her remark gave Mother an idea. "We'll invite them all back for a picnic. The Fourth of July would be a good time."

Annie was delighted. "We can have the picnic in the yard!"

Johnny turned a handspring, and the handspring gave Annie an idea. Her face lighted up.

"Let's have a surprise circus for everybody after the picnic dinner. Lyda wrote Mother that a big circus was coming to Cincinnati on the Fourth. Now she and Joe can see one after all!"

Johnny liked the idea. "I could be a strong man," he said. "You could do tricks on your pony, and Hulda could be a clown." Then his face darkened as a thought crossed his mind. "Do you think Hulda could keep a secret, Annie?"

Trumpet announced the Fourth of July with his loudest call. When the girls and their husbands arrived, the day was as bright as the stars in the flag Grandpap Shaw hung over the door.

The picnic under the big maple tree was the best ever. After dinner, the men pitched horseshoes. The big girls helped Mother with the dishes. Annie, Johnny, and Hulda disappeared.

Later, the grownups gathered in chairs under the shade of a tree.

"Where are those youngsters, anyhow?" asked Joe. "What are they up to?"

Mother smiled but said nothing.

At that moment, Annie rode out from behind Old Black's shed on her pony. "Ladies and gentlemen!" she called out. "We are proud to announce a great circus!"

Everyone clapped. Just then there was a terrible racket in the shed. Out ran Old Black's calf with Hulda on her back. For a second the startled audience thought this was the beginning of the circus.

The calf ran wildly toward the field. Hulda screamed and held on for dear life.

Quick as a flash, Annie streaked after her sister. Johnny, on his pony, flew after both of them.

Mother and the others jumped to their feet. Mother shut her eyes.

Lyda said, "It's going to be all right. Annie is heading the calf into a corner of the fence. Johnny is helping. There! Hulda is sliding off. She's safe!"

Johnny helped Hulda onto Annie's pony, then mounted his own. The ponies walked slowly back to the yard.

Everyone made a great fuss over Hulda. Finally the little girl said, "Annie and Johnny were afraid I couldn't keep the circus a secret.

146

Well, I had a secret of my own. I didn't even tell Annie and Johnny that I was going to ride in the parade, too."

Annie said, "You scared us all, Hulda. You did a dangerous thing. But at least I know you can keep a secret!"

"Thee can keep a secret too well," Mother said softly. Then she turned to the grownups. "Let's settle down and watch the real circus. A circus without Old Black's calf!"

"After that I want to tell you all about a secret that I've been keeping," said Grandpap Shaw. "I want to build a big, new house for my family."

Annie Goes into Business

IT WAS A FALL DAY when they moved into the new two-story log house. "Many hands make light work," Mother said.

By midmorning the furniture was all in place. Finally Annie hung her rifle up on the new pegs over the fireplace. "There," she said with satisfaction. "Now it's our very own new home."

Mr. Shaw looked around the house with pride. "Yes, it's home. We can't say it's 'our very own' just yet, though. I built the finest house I could for your mother and her family. She deserves the best. But I had to borrow a great deal of money from the bank. When the debt is paid off, then

149

we can say 'our very own.' If I don't pay the debt, the bank could take the house away from us."

Mr. Shaw saw that the children looked startled. "Don't worry. I have promised to pay the debt. As long as I have my job, I will give the bank a little money each month. It will take time, but the bank will not mind as long as I pay them some money each month, as I promised I would."

The children were relieved. Annie said, "I want to do something special for our first Thanksgiving in our new house." She took the rifle down from its pegs. She looped the thongs of the powder horn and the shot bag over her shoulder. "I don't know when I'll be back, but I hope I'll bring something with me."

Annie walked quickly and quietly through the woods. She didn't care what she found, but she wanted it to be something special. Suddenly she saw a feather on the ground. She almost stepped on it. It was chocolate brown. "I do believe it's a turkey feather! Wild turkeys look as though their tail feathers were dipped in chocolate."

She got down on her hands and knees. She peered along the ground ahead of her. "Yes, that's a turkey feather, all right. If my nose were as good as a dog's nose, I could tell how long it's been since the turkey went along here." She giggled at the idea of sniffing along a turkey trail. "I'll have to track him with my eyes instead of my nose. Maybe he hasn't gone far."

Annie's steps were as silent as an Indian's as she followed the turkey tracks. Suddenly the tracks stopped. There weren't any more any-where. Annie stood still, wondering what to do next. "I may have more chance of finding him if I stay right here," she decided. "He probably flew up in a tree where he's waiting for me to go away."

Annie sank down on a tree stump, her rifle on her knee. "Well, Mr. Gobbler," she thought, "I can be quiet and wait, too."

She sat as still as a stone. She would sit for a long time if necessary. She had heard of hunters who waited all day to get a shot at a gobbler. A turkey would be something special to take home for the Thanksgiving dinner. She must try to outsmart this smart bird.

Annie's eyes were the only part of her that moved. She looked up into the big oak in front of her. There, on one of the lower branches, was the turkey! Annie's keen eyes saw the brown of his slim body against the brown of the tree bark. His bluish head stood out like a scrap of blue sky.

Suddenly the turkey spread his great wings in flight. Quick as lightning Annie had the gun in her hands. She pulled the trigger. Down tumbled the gobbler!

Annie picked him up by his long legs. "I

thought maybe I wouldn't find you for hours," she said. "I was lucky. Now we'll have plenty of time to cook that special supper. Mr. Gobbler, you've given us a real Thanksgiving feast!"

Everybody enjoyed Thanksgiving that year. Mother said they all had much to be thankful for, and Annie knew that was true. She was happy just to be home with her own family.

One morning shortly afterward, Annie got ready to go hunting again. When she went to the kitchen, Mother looked at her and smiled.

"When thee stays at home helping me, thee looks like a young lady," Mother said. "When thee goes hunting, thee looks like a boy."

Annie looked down at herself. She made a comical face. Her scuffed shoes were too big for her slender feet. They were hand-me-downs from Johnny. Annie had stuffed paper in the toes of the shoes so they would not rub her feet. Her rough, woollen clothes were puckered with burrs. She had braided her thick chestnut hair tight so it would not get caught in the brambles. Now she pulled on an old cap of Johnny's.

"No one is going to see me but the birds," Annie said. "They may have fine feathers, but I don't need to be dressed up today."

Mother nodded. Annie was as pretty as a picture, even in her shabby clothes. All Mother said was, "As long as thee has such pink cheeks and bright eyes, thee looks all right to me."

Annie went hunting almost every day. She was as gay as a meadowlark. She wandered through the frosted fields and the woods with her gun on her shoulder. The countryside was quiet with the hush of coming winter.

Annie did not see another wild turkey that fall. "It's funny how easy it was to get that gobbler," she thought. "Too easy!"

She made up games to play while she was hunting. Sometimes she took a quick, running start. Sometimes when she saw a grouse rise, she whirled around once, twice, or even three times before firing. At first birds often soared out of sight, but Annie grew more and more skillful at wing shots. More and more often she brought her flying targets to the ground.

"Just swing with the bird," she would say to herself. "When it feels right, pull." There was double satisfaction in bringing home game she had brought down with her trick shots.

One night Annie's mother met her with bad news. Mother stepped outside and shut the door behind her. "I want to tell thee something before thee goes in," she said. "Your stepfather's eyes have got much worse. They have been growing dimmer for a long time. Today he had to give up his job because he can hardly see."

"Poor Grandpap Shaw!" Annie said quickly.

"Yes, poor man. What worries him most is that he can no longer take care of us."

"He mustn't worry about us!" Annie exclaimed. "Now we will take care of him."

"That's my good girl," Mother answered. "Still, where the money is to come from I don't know. We need money for the debt on the house."

The house! What if they lost the house to the bank! When she went in, Annie tried to be cheerful, but her heart was heavy.

That night after Hulda was asleep, Annie slipped out of bed. She wrapped up in a blanket and stood by the window a long time.

"It's up to me to do something," she thought. "Tag has the regular chores to do. Hulda is still too young to work, and Mother will want to stay home and look after Grandpap Shaw. It's up to me to earn money—but how?"

Outside, Annie saw the North Star glimmering cold and white over the dark line of the woods. It looked calm and serene, and seemed far away from the troubles that kept her awake. Annie remembered a verse she used to say long ago. She looked up at the star and murmured almost to herself,

> "Star light, star bright,
>   First star I see tonight,
>   I wish I may, I wish I might
>   Have the wish I wish tonight."

"I wish I could think of some way to help," she said aloud.

Suddenly she had an idea. "Of course!" she said out loud. "Why didn't I think of it before?"

When she crawled shivering into bed her plans were made.

Before sunup the next morning, Annie was outdoors with her rifle. By breakfast time she had four beautiful quail. She wrapped them carefully in damp swamp grass. Then she hid them under the rail fence before she went into the house.

At breakfast she was as cheerful as a chickadee. Her mother looked at her questioningly, but Annie just said, "I'm going into town for a while. I'll tell you all about it when I come back, Mother."

The ponies had been sold by this time, so Annie walked to Greenville. She went straight to the General Store. Mr. Katzenberger, the owner, smiled at the earnest little girl who wanted to do business with him. Annie carefully unwrapped layers of marsh grass. When Mr. Katzenberger saw the plump, feathered birds, his eyes brightened.

"I used only one shot for each," Annie told him quickly.

Mr. Katzenberger nodded. "I don't think we can sell them here in Greenville," he said. "People around here shoot their own birds. We might sell them in Cincinnati, though. I know a man there who will pay good prices for birds shot as

cleanly as these. His name is Jack Frost, and he runs the Bevis House, the best hotel in town."

Before Annie left, she and the store owner had agreed on a plan. Annie would put her game in baskets. She was to hand them to the mail carrier when he reached the crossroad near her house. The carrier would take them to Mr. Katzenberger. Mr. Katzenberger would ship them to Cincinnati each day.

"It will be good business for both of us," he said. He reached over the counter and shook Annie's hand on their new venture. Annie's small hand was swallowed up in his big fist.

The family was delighted when Annie told her news that evening. Annie was delighted, too. "Just think! I'll get paid for doing what I like most!" she said, dancing around the kitchen.

It would take a long time to pay off the debt to the bank. Annie knew that, but she was sure she could do it, bit by bit. She wouldn't take time off for anything. Not to visit Lyda! Not to go to school! Reading and writing would have to wait. Now hunting was more important. It was the most important thing of all.

During the next few years, news of Annie's skill with her rifle began to spread. Before long it spread all over Darke County.

"Yes siree," Mr. Katzenberger often told his customers. "Anything you hear about how that little girl can shoot is true. Mr. Jack Frost's customers in Cincinnati are flocking in to eat Annie's quail. There's no scattered shot in those birds for people to break their teeth on! One shot through the head and that's all. She's the surest shot I know."

When the men around the warm stove in Mr. La Motte's store asked about Annie, the Frenchman would beam. His red beard bobbed up and down as he talked.

"Little Miss Mozee? Yes, she comes in here to

get her supplies. She pays me with game. If you old-timers aren't careful, she's going to outshoot all of you. She's got eyes like a hawk. She's as quick as a deer, too! She's just a young thing— thirteen, fourteen maybe—but she's fast growing up to be a young lady."

Before she was fifteen, Annie made the last payment at the bank. Proudly she carried home the paper that said the debt was paid.

Mother's eyes were bright with tears as she read it. "Thee is our big girl, Annie."

"This is our house for always, our very own," Annie said. She gave each member of the family a hug. Then she grabbed Johnny and made him waltz with her around the room.

An Expert
Comes to Town

ANNIE BURST INTO the house full of excitement. "Mother, Mother! Here's a letter just for me! Isn't that my name on the envelope?"

Annie's mother took the letter over to the lamp. "Yes, it says, 'Miss Annie Moses.'"

"I can read my own name, but you'll have to read the letter to me," Annie said. "Quick. Who in the world can be writing to me?"

Mother looked at the postmark. "It's from Cincinnati, and it looks like thy sister's handwriting," she said. "Yes, here on the back it says, 'From Mrs. Joseph Stein.'"

Mother settled down in her rocker. Annie hung

over her shoulder. She looked at the writing. "What does Lyda say? Read it quickly."

Annie's mother started to read aloud in her gentle voice.

" 'Dear Little Sister—I guess, though, you aren't so little any more, now that you've turned sixteen. Joe and I want to give you a birthday present. We have decided that the best present would be a trip to the big city.' "

Annie caught her breath. "Does she mean Cincinnati, Mother?" she asked.

Her mother nodded and read on.

" 'If you come to live with us here for a while, there are all sorts of things you can learn. You can learn how to read and write, and how to sketch or play the piano. You're the one who can learn anything you want to. I've always said to Joe that you were different from other girls— quicker and more clever and more full of life somehow.' "

Mother looked up, smiling. "Is thee blushing at all the compliments, Annie?"

Annie's face was pink, but she just grinned and said, "Go on."

" 'Together you and I could make some pretty dresses for you to wear. Now that you are almost a young lady, you will want to dress like one, and not have thorns and prickles in your skirts, the way you do when you go hunting.' "

Quickly Annie glanced down at her skirt. Sure enough, it was full of burrs. She pulled at one and made a funny face.

Mother kept on reading. " 'You have already done your share—and more—in helping the home folk. We don't want you to spend all the rest of your life in the woods like a wild turkey. I know you love the country, but you can learn to love the city, too. All this time you've been sending your birds to Cincinnati. Now it's time for you to come yourself. I've already started prettying up the spare room for you. Ask Mother to write us when we should meet you at the station. Your loving sister, Lyda.

" 'P.S. Joe wants me to be sure to tell you that Cincinnati is full of shooting clubs and shooting galleries. There will be shooting matches to see, too. He doesn't want you to get homesick.' "

Mother stopped reading and looked at Annie with a twinkle in her eye. "Well, Annie, what does thee think of Lyda's birthday present?"

Annie let out a big sigh as though she had been holding her breath a long time. "It will be exciting. I'll be glad to visit Lyda and Joe, and to learn to read at last!"

Annie looked around the snug house. Then she added, "I'll hate to leave you and Grandpap Shaw and Hulda. And how I'll miss Tag!"

At that moment the door flew open and Johnny came in, just in time to hear Annie's last words. "Miss me?" he asked. "Where are you going?"

When it had been explained to him, he looked disappointed. He hated to be left behind. Then he grinned. "It's a good thing Lyda doesn't want me to learn city manners and wear city clothes! I'd rather take care of things here, Annie."

Mother said, "This will always be thy home, Annie. Thee can always come back when thee wants to."

Annie gave her mother a big hug. "Thank you, Mother," she said. "I'll always want to come back, too. You know that."

"Now," Mother said briskly. "We must plan a new dress for thee to wear. Lyda isn't the only one who knows how a young lady should look."

With Mother's help, Annie got ready to go. For several days the house was a busy place, but at last everything was in readiness. New clothes were packed. Annie was scrubbed, and her long chestnut hair was brushed and combed.

"We will miss thee, Annie," Mother said the

morning Annie was to leave. "I don't know what we would have done without thee. But I'm glad that thee will at last have a chance to go to school and to see something besides the woods and fields here at home."

Annie looked around the kitchen that she knew so well. "I'll miss you," she said. "I'll miss everybody, but—I'm glad to be going, too."

Grandpap Shaw and Johnny took her to the station to meet the train. Late that afternoon Joe and Lyda met her at the station in Cincinnati. Annie was amazed by the bustle and noise of the streets. She was amazed by the endless rows of buildings and houses along the streets, and by the countless people she saw wherever she went.

"Where do they all come from?" she wondered. "What can they all do?"

One day Joe said, "Annie, how would you like to go downtown tonight? You've been here almost a week now, working hard at your reading lessons. I think it's time you saw some more of the city, don't you?"

"I'd love to go," Annie said. "I've already seen a lot from the top of your hill here—all of Fairmount where you live, the Ohio River, and the part of the city called Oakley. That's a pretty name—Oakley."

"Oh, you've just had a bird's eye view," Lyda said. "We could ride the horsecars all the way downtown. It's such fun to ride in streetcars pulled by horses. All the lights, the crowds, the music, and the hotels are downtown."

"Could we go to Mr. Jack Frost's hotel?" Annie asked.

"The Bevis House? Surely," Joe answered. "Come on, girls, get your hats."

Annie put on her new pink hat. How strange to wear a hat every time one went out of the house! Even when it wasn't cold or raining!

"My, you look nice!" Lyda said. Joe agreed.

Annie looked into the mirror. She giggled. "Well, I guess this hat is prettier than Tag's old cap that I used to wear."

When the horsecar arrived downtown, Joe was the first one off. He gave his arm to Lyda, who stepped down like a fine lady. Then he turned to help Annie. She had already jumped down to the ground.

Annie was glad to walk between Joe and Lyda as they started down the street. How crowded the sidewalks were! How dazzling the lights! And how gay the band music sounded! German waltzes poured from several windows. Annie felt like dancing.

"Here's the hotel, Annie. Come on, we'll go in and see if Jack Frost is here."

Suddenly Annie felt shy. She hadn't dreamed that her quail had come to a place as fine as this! Mr. Frost had liked the quail, but what would he think when he found out his hunter was a girl? Annie touched her pink hat for courage, then followed Joe and Lyda inside.

Soon she was shaking hands with a tall, friendly man behind a desk in the hotel. Joe was saying, "Mr. Frost, here is your hunter from Darke County, Miss Annie Moses."

"Well, well, Miss Annie! I've heard a lot about you from our friend, Mr. Katzenberger, in Greenville," Mr. Frost said with a smile. "He didn't tell me that one of the best shots in Ohio looked like a pink wild rose, however."

Annie blushed. For once she couldn't think of a word to say.

Mr. Frost went on. "I hope you like it here in our city." He turned to Joe. "Have you taken her to the Coliseum yet to see Frank Butler's shooting tricks? Butler is one of the best shots in the country, you know. He's staying here at the hotel."

Without pausing for breath, Mr. Frost continued, "He's been trying to find someone who will have a shooting contest with him. So far he hasn't found anyone good enough." Frost stopped and looked at Annie as though he had just thought of something that surprised him. He turned to Joe.

"An unknown little miss from the country shooting against the famous Frank Butler! What a match that would be! How about it? What do you think? Do you think she could do it?"

By the time Annie realized what was happening, Joe and Mr. Frost were busy making plans. "We won't tell him it's a young girl," Frost said. "We'll just say an expert has come to town. Now, where shall we have the shooting match?"

Lyda spoke up. "Why don't you have the match at the shooting club in Fairmount? That's near home."

Joe nodded. "Yes, at Shooter's Hill."

"All right. That's settled," said Frost. "All

that's left to do now is to get Frank Butler to agree to the match."

Annie had stood by all this time, listening to what was said. "How about me?" she finally asked, and she sounded almost angry.

Mr. Frost and Joe and Lyda stared at her in surprise. She was standing as tall and straight as she could. She held her head high. Her gray eyes were snapping-bright. She looked steadily at Mr. Frost.

Mr. Frost came out from behind the desk. He made a bow. "I'm sorry, Miss Annie. You're right. I'll ask you now. Do you agree to shoot in a match with Mr. Frank Butler?"

Annie took a deep breath. She said slowly, "I agree." Then she laughed. "To tell the truth, I can hardly wait."

A New Name

ANNIE DID NOT have long to wait. It was a bright Thanksgiving day when she started up to Shooter's Hill with Joe and Lyda.

On the way, Joe explained the rules of the match. Annie and Butler would take turns shooting until each had shot twenty-five times. The targets would be clay pigeons, Joe said.

"Clay pigeons?" Annie asked.

Joe explained, "They're just called pigeons. They really look more like saucers. When you're ready to shoot, you call, 'Pull!' You can't raise your gun until then. The target will fly up in the air. If you hit it, the referee will call,

'Dead bird.' You never know which direction the clay saucers will go. That's what makes it hard," he said. "You have to watch closely."

"That won't be hard," Annie said. "At home I never knew which directions the real birds were going to fly, either."

"That's it," Joe said, patting her shoulder. "Just pretend you're back home shooting quail and you won't have any trouble."

"Does the winner get a turkey?" Annie asked, remembering the only shoot she had seen.

Joe laughed. "The prize, young lady, is one hundred dollars."

"Oh," said Annie in a small voice.

Lyda spoke up. "Maybe you'd better pretend it's just a turkey."

This time Annie laughed. "While I'm at it, maybe I'd better pretend I'm not even me. It won't be hard to do. Everything is so strange I don't feel much like Annie Moses any more.

I don't know who I am, but I'm beginning to feel like a new and different person."

"Well, you look different," Lyda said. She glanced with pride at the new blue dress Annie had made. "Just the same, I hope you'll always be our Annie."

"Yes, I'll be your Annie all right, but I'd like to be Annie Somebody Else, too," Annie said. She wrinkled her forehead, thinking. She stopped a minute to look out over the city. What was it Lyda had called that neighborhood near her home? "I know!" she said aloud. "Oakley, Annie Oakley. That would be a nice new name!"

"Say, that isn't bad," Joe said in approval.

As they entered the grounds of the shooting club, they heard gay music. The band was playing a lively march. Overhead, a flag snapped in the breeze. A large holiday crowd had already gathered to watch the match.

Mr. Frost came over to greet Joe and Lyda and

Annie. "Ah, there you are, Miss Annie," he said. "I knew I could depend on you. Come now, I want you to meet Mr. Butler."

Before she knew it, Annie was looking up at a tall man who smiled down on her. She thought he was the handsomest man she had ever seen. Mr. Frost said simply, "Miss Annie, this is Frank Butler."

Mr. Butler tipped his hat. It was soft green and had a perky feather. "How do, Missie," he said and held out his hand. "Have you come to watch me shoot?" he asked. "I hope you won't be disappointed."

"I don't expect to be," Annie said, smiling.

Frank Butler turned to Mr. Frost. "It's about time to begin. Where is this expert you've been telling me about?"

Frost grinned. "Right here. It's Miss Annie. She's the crack shot from Darke County."

Butler stared at the slim young girl in surprise. "Are you really?" he asked.

"Sure as shootin'," Annie said.

Butler was delighted. He led Annie to the shooting station. He had his own gun with him. Annie chose one from a nearby rack. It felt good to hold a gun again.

Someone tossed a coin to see who would shoot first. Frank Butler won.

"Pull," he called. The clay saucer flew into the air. Frank shattered it.

"Dead bird!" called the referee.

Now it was Annie's turn. Suddenly she was frightened. Everybody was watching her. Everybody was waiting to see what she could do.

Then she remembered what Joe had said— "Just pretend you're home, shooting quail."

Suddenly her fear was gone. She imagined she was back in the woods and fields of Darke County. In a clear voice she called, "Pull!"

A pigeon flew up. *Crack!* went Annie's gun.

"Dead bird!" called the referee.

First Frank and then Annie shot. Neither missed a single clay pigeon.

The crowd liked the tall, handsome man and the pretty, young girl with braids! She seemed as graceful and as quick as a hummingbird! .

Finally it was Frank Butler's last turn. He cried, "Pull!" and raised his gun as the clay pigeon shot into the air. This time he missed.

"Missed!" the referee called.

A kind of groan rose from the crowd. Then all eyes were fastened on Annie as she stepped forward into the shooting station.

She took a deep breath. Here was her chance. "Pull!" she cried.

There was a loud *Crack!*

"Dead bird!" the referee called.

Sounds of clapping came to Annie's ears. She looked around, surprised. She had forgotten where she was. She had forgotten about the crowd. She had almost forgotten Frank Butler.

Quickly he came over and held out his hand. "Congratulations, Missie. I'm proud to lose to an expert like you." He looked as though he meant it. "You must come to see my shooting act in the Coliseum. I think you might enjoy it."

"Thank you. I'd like to come," Annie said.

Frank looked pleased. "What did you say your name is?" he asked.

Annie's eyes lighted up with mischief. She tilted her chin a little higher. "It's Annie," she said. "Annie Oakley."

Little Sure Shot

So ANNIE MOSES from Darke County gave herself a new name. It was not long before she acquired another new name, too—Mrs. Frank Butler.

Frank Butler had not only been delighted to shoot against the slim girl with the gray eyes and chestnut-colored hair. As he talked with her and watched her that autumn day, he had fallen in love. About a year after the shooting match, he wrote Annie a letter asking her to marry him.

Annie agreed at once. Then began a wandering life as Annie traveled about the country with Frank and his partner. Each day in the theater she watched the act. Each night, in their room at the hotel, with Frank's help, she studied. She learned to read and write, then studied all the other things she had wanted to know.

One day Frank's partner fell ill and was unable to go on stage. Annie was worried.

"What will you do, Frank?" she asked. "Can you do the whole act alone?"

"No," Frank said, smiling and shaking his head. "But I don't have to go on alone. You'll go on with me. There's nothing to it, Annie. You know the act, and you can shoot as well as either of us can. We'll get along fine."

That night Annie Oakley appeared on stage for the first time. When Frank announced her name and held up a target for her to shoot at, she ran on stage. She took a rifle from the stand, aimed, fired — and missed!

Surprised, Annie studied the lights quickly and fired again. This time there was no mistake.

From that day on the act became Frank Butler and Annie Oakley. As the years passed, Frank pushed Annie more and more to the front. A woman sharpshooter was new and different then, and people enjoyed watching her. Frank was proud to let the world see how good she was.

One night the great Indian chief Sitting Bull was taken to a theater where Frank and Annie were playing. He sat bored and disinterested until Annie ran on the stage. Suddenly, as she hit target after target without fail, he sprang excitedly to his feet. "Little Sure Shot!" he cried. "She's a little sure shot!" So Annie acquired a third name—Little Sure Shot—which stayed with her all the rest of her life.

A few years later, Frank and Annie joined Buffalo Bill's Wild West Show. Annie was the star and the only white woman in the show.

In 1886 the show opened on the night before Thanksgiving at Madison Square Garden in New

184

York City. Thousands of people were there. They had come to see Buffalo Bill. They had come to see the Indians, cowboys, and Mexicans. They had come to see Little Sure Shot.

Suddenly Buffalo Bill rode into the ring on his beautiful dappled horse. He was a tall man with a pointed white beard and long white hair under a wide-brimmed hat.

"Ladies and gentlemen!" he cried in a booming voice. "The Wild West presents the first and greatest show of western life and history!"

Into the arena came a long parade—whooping Indians, yelling cowboys on galloping horses, buffaloes, and a swaying stagecoach. Then, just as suddenly as they had come, they were gone. For a moment everything was still.

Then Buffalo Bill spoke again. "Ladies and gentlemen, the Wild West presents the beautiful girl of the western plains, Little Sure Shot, the one and only Annie Oakley!"

A small graceful woman raced into view on a western pony. The spotlight had a hard time keeping up with her. Suddenly she stopped, wheeled her horse, and swept off her hat, a wide-brimmed hat pinned with a silver star. Then she turned and made the pony dance lightly into the center of the arena.

At that moment a cowboy galloped past her with several targets fastened to the end of a leather thong. As he passed her, Annie leaned from the saddle, grabbed up a pistol from the ground, and broke each target with a quick shot.

Next a fiery wheel was spun. Six circling candle flames were snuffed out by six fast shots.

Then Annie jumped to the ground. Like a wild deer, she leaped over a gun stand. A man tossed six glass balls into the air. Annie picked up three guns, one after another. She broke two balls with the first gun, two with the second gun, and the last two with the third gun.

"An attendant will now hold a playing card as a target," the announcer said. "Miss Oakley will turn her back on it. She will look at the reflection of the target in the bright blade of a hunting knife. Then, aiming back over her shoulder, she will hit the center of the card."

People held their breath. *Crack!* went Annie's rifle. The card fell to the ground with a hole through the center. A great "O-o-o-h!" went up from the audience, then a cheer.

Annie made a quick little bow, leaped on her pony and galloped around the arena once more. Without slowing for a moment, she slid head-down from the saddle and tied a scarf above one of the pony's flying hoofs. In a twinkling she stood up in the saddle. As she galloped off, she waved her big hat to the thunder of the crowd's applause.

"Annie Oakley!" people shouted. "Hurrah for Little Sure Shot!"

A Letter Home

"The Wild West,"
Earl's Court,
London, England,
May, 1887.

Dear Family,

Today your Annie was presented to the Queen of England!

The Queen asked if we would give a special performance for her and her guests. This is Victoria's Jubilee Year, you know. Everybody is celebrating her fifty years on the throne.

She has lots of visitors here from other lands—kings and queens, and princes and princesses—

all kinds of grand folks. They all wanted to see our Wild West Show.

They all arrived at the show grounds in fine carriages. You should have seen the glittering uniforms and beautiful dresses and the high-stepping horses! They made almost as fine a sight as our Wild West parade, except that they didn't ride so fast. They didn't whoop and holler like our Indians and cowboys, either.

My shooting was first on the program after the parade. For a minute I was a little nervous. I haven't been nervous since my match on Shooter's Hill years ago. But then, I've never before shot in front of the Queen of England!

I took a quick look at the Queen. She didn't have a crown on her head at all—just a little black bonnet almost like Mother's go-to-meeting bonnet. That made me feel right at home. So I just went ahead and hit flying targets and balls and wheels of fire as fast as ever. The royal visitors clapped hardest when I shot a dime from between Frank's fingers. When I bowed and rode off, the Prince of Wales yipped like a cowboy.

After the show was over, the queen asked to meet me. You will be pleased to know that I made her a proper curtsey. She gave me a present, a beautiful pair of opera glasses. She pinned a medal on my buckskin jacket. Then she said— and you'll never believe this—"You are a very clever girl." And I thought I was grown up!

Later that afternoon I changed into a new dress I had made. It's a pretty muslin dress lined with pale blue silk. On the lawn in front of my tent I gave a tea party. Some of the royal children came to the party.

At first they were shy and stiff, but I showed them the beaded moccasins and feathered war bonnet that Sitting Bull gave me. I let them play with my big collection of medals. Then they chattered like children at a party back home. I think their mothers were surprised that a girl from the wild and woolly West knew how to serve tea!

When the show closes here at the end of the summer, Frank and I will go to Germany. The German Crown Prince has invited me to come and do some shooting for the Emperor. Later we will go to Paris for a while.

Tell Frenchy La Motte that I will send him a postcard from France. After France, we'll go to Italy. At least I am learning geography!

In your last letter you asked if I ever get homesick. Sometimes I do, but not so often now—not since Frank taught me how to write. A letter is almost as good as a visit. Someday I'll come home to Darke County for a real visit, sure as shooting.

Besides, I want to see if I can still track down a wild turkey and bring him home for supper.

Your loving

Annie